Finn couldn't be left in the dark. He had to know what they were facing. "What's the matter?"

The doctor smiled up at him. "Nothing at all. You're having twins."

"Twins!"

Holly said it at the same time as Finn.

"Yes, see here." The doctor showed them both babies.

It was the most amazing thing Finn had ever witnessed in his life. Twins. Who'd have thought? His vision started to blur, causing him to blink repeatedly. He was going to be a father.

He glanced down at Holly. A tear streamed down her cheek. His gut clenched. Was that a sign of joy or unhappiness? It was hard for him to tell. And then she turned and smiled at him. He released the pent-up breath in his lungs.

"Finn, are you okay?"

He glanced up, finding that he was alone with Holly. "Okay? No."

Her lips formed an O. "Can I say or do anything?"

He shook his head. He should be the one reassuring *her*, letting her know this was all going to be all right, but he couldn't lie to her. He had no idea how any of this was going to be all right. He was the last person in the world who should be a father. In fact, up until this point, he'd intended to leave all his estate to designated charities.

But now... Wow, everything had just changed.

Dear Reader,

Sometimes in order to go forward you must first go backwards—to face down the memories that have defined so much of your life.

It isn't easy—not by a long shot. Whether you try moving forward or back, you may find yourself stuck. And so it is for my hero and heroine. What they don't understand yet is that the act of helping each other will open up their hearts and allow them to make peace with the past.

One very special night, sexy billionaire Finn Lockwood finds himself alone in his office when in walks paralegal Holly Abrams. She's fun and engaging, making him forget all the reasons he's still a bachelor. However, when things go further than either of them intended they mutually agree not to complicate matters further and go their separate ways.

But sometimes actions can't be undone—no matter how hard each person tries. Actions have consequences. And when it's love from the get-go—there's no going back. The heart has a will of its own.

So as the holiday season rolls around Finn's and Holly's paths are destined to cross again. Will they be able to help each other undo the damage from Christmas past? And will they be able to face the ghosts of Christmas present in order to have a Christmas future?

Happy reading,

Jennifer

HER
FESTIVE BABY
BOMBSHELL

BY
JENNIFER FAYE

Published in Great Britain 2016
By Mills & Boon, an imprint of HarperCollins*Publishers*
1 London Bridge Street, London, SE1 9GF

ISBN: 978-0-263-06549-7

Our policy is to use papers that are natural, renewable and recyclable
products and made from wood grown in sustainable forests. The logging
and manufacturing processes conform to the legal environmental
regulations of the country of origin.

Printed and bound in Great Britain
by CPI Antony Rowe, Chippenham, Wiltshire

Award-winning author **Jennifer Faye** pens fun, heartwarming romances. Jennifer has won the RT Reviewers' Choice Best Book Award, is a Top Pick author and has been nominated for numerous awards. Now living her dream, she resides with her patient husband, one amazing daughter—the other remarkable daughter is off chasing her own dreams—and two spoiled cats. She'd love to hear from you via her website: jenniferfaye.com.

Books by Jennifer Faye

Mills & Boon Romance

Brides for the Greek Tycoons
The Greek's Nine-Month Surprise
The Greek's Ready-Made Wife

The Vineyards of Calanetti
Return of the Italian Tycoon

The DeFiore Brothers
The Playboy of Rome
Best Man for the Bridesmaid

Rancher to the Rescue
Snowbound with the Soldier
Safe in the Tycoon's Arms
The Return of the Rebel
A Princess by Christmas
The Prince's Christmas Vow

Visit the Author Profile page at millsandboon.co.uk for more titles.

For Nancy F.
To a wonderful lady that I'm honored to know.
Thanks so much for the encouragement.

PROLOGUE

Lockwood International Offices, New York City

"WHAT ARE YOU doing here?" a rich, deep voice called out from the shadows of the executive suite.

Holly Abrams froze. The breath caught in her throat. The pounding of her heart echoed in her ears. She searched the darkness for the mysterious man.

And then he stepped into the light. She immediately recognized him. It was the CEO of Lockwood International, Finn Lockwood. The air whooshed from her lungs.

This wasn't the first time their paths had crossed, but they weren't by any stretch of the imagination what you would consider friends. And he didn't sound the least bit happy to see her, but then again, why should he?

When her gaze met his, her palms grew damp. "Hi." Why did her voice have to be so soft—so seductive? She swallowed hard.

"Isn't it a bit late for you to be working?"

Overtime was nothing new to Holly. After a failed engagement, she'd sworn off men and instead focused all of her energy on her career. When she was working, she felt confident and driven.

"I...uh, have these papers for you." She held out the large manila envelope to him. "I was told you wanted this contract right away." When he went to retrieve the envelope, their fingers brushed. A jolt of awareness arched between them. The sensation zinged up her arm and settled in her chest.

"Thank you." As the seconds ticked by, he asked, "Is there something else you need?"

Need? Her gaze dipped to his lips—his very kissable lips.

She remembered their last meeting in the elevator. They'd been alone when she'd dropped a slip of paper. They'd simultaneously bent over to retrieve it, bringing their faces so close. When they'd straightened, he'd stared at her as though seeing her as a woman instead of as a paralegal in Lockwood's legal department. She knew when a man was interested in her, but when the elevator dinged and the doors slid open, the moment had passed. It had left her wondering if it'd been a product of wishful thinking on her part.

And now, before she made a further fool of herself, she needed to make a speedy exit. "I'll just let you deal with that." She turned to retrace her footsteps back to the elevator when she remembered her manners. She glanced over her shoulder. "Good night."

"Wait."

With her back to him, she inwardly groaned. Her gaze moved to the elevator at the end of the hallway. Her escape was so close and yet so far away. Suppressing a resigned sigh, she turned.

"Come with me." Without waiting for her response, he strode into his office.

What in the world did he want with her? Her black peep-toe platform pumps echoed as she crossed the marble floor. She couldn't tell which was louder, the *click-click* of her heels or the *thump-thump* of her heart. Most people didn't make her nervous, but Mr. Lockwood was the exception.

When Holly entered the spacious office, she had to admit she was awed. While he read over the document, she took in her surroundings. Behind Mr. Lockwood's desk stood a wall of windows. Being so high up, it provided the most amazing view of Manhattan. She longed to rush over and stare out at the bustling city, but she didn't dare.

The sound of a desk drawer opening distracted her. Mr. Lockwood appeared to be searching for something. While he was preoccupied, she continued her visual tour of his office. It reminded her of a museum with its impressive sculptures as well as a baseball collection ensconced in glass cases. But the bookcases spanning an entire wall were what drew her in.

She struggled not to gape at the large collection of books. He liked to read. They had that in common. She wanted to slip across the room and examine the titles, but when she glanced over at Mr. Lockwood, he pointed to one of the two chairs in front of his desk. Without a word, she complied.

"What do you think of the office?"

"It's very nice." She indicated the floor-to-ceiling bookcases. "Have you read them all?"

"I have. And what about you? Do you like to read?"

"Oh, yes." She laced her fingers together to keep from fidgeting with the hem of her skirt. "I read every chance I get."

"Is that why you're not downstairs at the company's fiftieth anniversary celebration? Would you prefer to be at home reading?"

Was this some sort of test? She hesitated. Was there a right and a wrong answer? Her clasped hands tightened as his gaze probed her. Could he tell how nervous his presence made her?

"I missed the party because I needed to finish the contract." She indicated the document on his desk. "I was just going to leave it for you before I headed home." She wasn't the only one not attending the party. What was his excuse for skipping his own celebration? "I figured you'd be at the party."

"I already made a brief appearance. No one will let their guard down around the boss so I made a quick exit, letting everyone get back to having a good time."

She could totally understand people being nervous around him. He was an intense man, who insisted on only the best from his employees. "That can't be much fun for you."

He shrugged. "I'm fine with it."

She looked at him in a new light, realizing for the first time that the privilege of working up here in this ivory tower was also a sentence of isolation. "It doesn't seem right that you're working instead of celebrating your family's accomplishments."

He shook his head. "This is the way it must be."

Well, now, that was an odd comment. It was on the tip of her tongue to question him about it, but she thought better of it. She had a feeling his pleasantness had its limitations.

Quietness settled over the room as Mr. Lockwood scanned the twenty-one-page document. Holly struggled to sit still—waiting and wondering why he wanted her to remain there. Her index finger repeatedly smoothed over the chipped nail polish on her thumb.

There was something about this man that turned her into a mass of jittery nerves. But what? It wasn't his billions or his power. It was something more intrinsic, but she couldn't quite put her finger on it.

"This exhibit isn't right." He gestured to a page in the contract. "Do you have your source material?"

"Not on me. But I double-checked everything." In actuality, she'd quadruple-checked the figures, but she didn't want to sound like she'd been trying too hard to impress him.

His brows drew together into a formidable line. "You had to have made a mistake. This doesn't make sense."

"Prove it." The words slipped past her lips before she could stop them.

Mr. Lockwood's eyes widened as though unaccustomed to being challenged. She continued to hold his gaze. She wasn't going to back down—not when the one thing she greatly valued was in question—her reputation.

"These exhibits are skewed. I'm positive of it." His eyes darkened. "I'll log in to the system and then you can show me where you pulled your numbers."

For the next hour they worked side by side, going over the figures in the exhibits. In the end the contract was wrong, but to Holly's relief, it hadn't been her fault. The numbers on one of the source files had been transposed. After printing a revised copy, Finn signed it. Holly used his personal assistant's scanner to email the contract to the designated party.

"Thanks for the assistance." Finn slipped the hard copy back into the envelope. "Sorry to take up so much of your evening and for causing you to miss dinner." He glanced at his Rolex. "We'll have to remedy that."

"That's okay. It's not a big deal."

"I insist on dinner." He stood and then moved around the desk. "You did me a big favor tonight by helping with the contract." His gaze dipped to her lips before quickly returning to her face. The corners of his mouth lifted into a sexy smile. "And I'd like to show you how thankful I am for the help with meeting that deadline."

Oh, he definitely had more than dinner on his mind. The thought sent a new wave of nervous tremors through her stomach. She glanced away. Her initial inclination was to turn him down. Her experience with men was less than impressive. But did that mean she had to live in solitude?

What was wrong with a little company? A little laughter and perhaps flirting? And maybe a little more. Her gaze met his once more. It'd all be fine as long as neither of them had any expectations. After all, it wasn't like it would ever happen again.

"Dinner sounds good."

"Great." He made a brief phone call and then turned to her. "It's all arranged. I'll just drop this envelope on Clara's desk and then we'll be off."

A little voice inside Holly said to be cautious. Finn Lockwood wasn't just any man and she knew nothing of his world. But another part of her was drawn to him like a moth to a flame—and boy, was he hot.

The sizzling tension smoldered between them as they quietly rode down in the elevator. When they stepped into the parking garage beneath the building there was a sleek black town car waiting for them. A driver immediately alighted and opened the door for them.

Holly climbed in first, followed by Finn. When he joined her, his muscular leg brushed against hers. Her stomach shivered with excitement. When their hands came to rest side by side on the leather seat, neither pulled away. It felt as though the interior of the car was statically charged. Every nerve ending tingled with anticipation.

As the car eased into the Friday evening traffic, she glanced over at Finn. She was surprised to find him staring back at her. Her heart *thump-thumped*, loud and fast.

"Where to, sir?" the driver asked.

"The penthouse." Finn's darkened gaze returned to Holly. "I thought we would dine in. Unless, of course, you have something else in mind."

She had something on her mind, but it wasn't food. Perhaps she had been spending too much time working these days because there had to be a reasonable explanation for her lack of common sense. Because all she could think about was how much she longed to press her lips to his.

CHAPTER ONE

Seven weeks later...

BAH, HUMBUG...

Finn Lockwood didn't care if the saying was cliché. It was how he felt. Even though this was the first week after Thanksgiving, the holiday festivities were in full swing. He wanted no part of having a holly jolly Christmas. Even though he'd turned off the speakers in his office, the music still crept down the hallway, taunting him with its joyous melody.

He did his utmost to block out the mocking words. Instead, he focused on the stack of papers awaiting his signature. He was so close to being out of here—out of the office—out of New York City.

"I just love this." His longtime assistant, Clara, strode into his office with a hefty stack of papers.

"Love what? The endless phone calls and this mess of paperwork?"

"Um, no." Color filled her cheeks as she placed the papers on his desk. "I meant this song, 'Home for the Holidays.' It puts me in a warm fuzzy mood."

His pen hovered over the document as he paused to listen. The sentimental words about home and family stabbed at his scarred heart. "To each his own."

She swept her dark bobbed hair behind her ear. "Although it never feels like the holiday season until that first snowflake falls. Don't you think so?"

He frowned at her. "How long have you known me?"

"Almost eight years."

"And by now I'd have thought you'd realize I don't do holidays."

"I… I just keep hoping—"

"Don't. It's not going to happen." An awkward silence ensued as he glanced over a disbursement and then signed it.

"Oh. I almost forgot. These came for you." She handed over two tickets for the Mistletoe Ball.

He accepted the tickets. Without bothering to look at them, he slipped them in a side desk drawer with other tickets from years gone by. When he glanced back at his assistant, unspoken questions reflected in her eyes. "What?"

Clara hesitated, fidgeting with the pen in her hand. "Why do you order tickets every year but then never use them?"

"Don't you think it's a worthy cause?" When Clara nodded, he continued. "I want to do my part." His voice grew husky with emotion. "If everyone does their part, maybe they'll find a cure for leukemia. The damn disease steals lives far too soon." His hand tightened around the pen. "It leaves nothing but devastation in its wake."

Clara's eyes widened. "I… I agree. I, um, just can't afford the tickets."

Finn realized he'd said too much. No one knew he was the sole sponsor of the ball and that was the way he intended for it to remain. But he just couldn't attend—couldn't face the guilt. If it wasn't for him and his actions, his mother and father would still be alive. They'd be attending the ball each year just like they'd always done in years past.

Finn pulled open the desk drawer and removed the tickets. "Here. Take them. It'd be better if they were used rather than sitting around gathering dust."

Her gaze moved from the tickets to him. "But I couldn't. You should give them to someone else."

When she rattled off the names of people who headed up his various divisions and departments, he said, "I want you to have them."

"Thank you." She accepted the tickets with a hesitant smile.

"Now back to business. I hope this is the last of what I need to sign because we have a trip to prepare for."

"A trip? When?"

"Tomorrow morning." This wasn't the first time he'd sprung a spur-of-the-moment trip on her. "And I'll need you there—"

"But..." Clara worried her bottom lip.

"But what? Surely you can reschedule anything on my calendar for some time after the first of the year."

"It's not that."

Color stained her cheeks as she glanced down at the tickets. She remained quiet, which was so unlike her. Something was definitely amiss and he didn't like it, not one little bit. They were set to leave in the morning for his private island in the Caribbean for a secret business meeting. When it concluded, Clara would return to New York while he remained in the sun and sand until after the New Year—when life returned to normal and people were no longer gushing with the holiday spirit.

Clara's continued silence worried him. He leaned back in his chair, taking in the worry lines bracketing her eyes. "What's the problem?"

"I got engaged last night." She held up her hand. A sparkly diamond now resided on her ring finger.

"Congratulations."

"Thank you."

"I'm sure you'll have lots of planning to do after our trip—"

"Well, um...that's the thing." Her gaze dipped again. "We're eloping this weekend."

"What?" She couldn't be serious. He had everything worked out. His business associates were meeting them on his private island in two days. "You can't back out on me now."

"I'm really sorry. But Steve, my fiancé, he, um...surprised me with tickets to fly to Vegas."

Finn resisted rolling his eyes. *Could things get any worse?* His plans had already hit a major snag, prompting this emergency meeting, and now his trusted employee was running off to Vegas to get hitched by some Elvis impersonator. *This is just great!*

"You can't bail on me." He raked his fingers through his hair. "I need your assistance for this meeting. It's important."

"Oh. Um…" She wrung her hands together.

He caught the shimmer of unshed tears in Clara's eyes. This was not good—not good at all. He was so used to having Clara at his beck and call that he hadn't anticipated this scenario. He hated being put in this position—choosing between his work and his associate's happiness. There had to be a compromise.

After a bit of thought, he conceded. "If you can find a suitable replacement, you can have the time off. But it'll have to be done pronto. My meeting can't be delayed."

Clara's eyes widened. "I'll get right on it. I'll have someone by this afternoon."

She turned and rushed out the door, leaving him alone to scowl about his plans being upended. Normally he'd have insisted on being involved in the selection of a temporary PA, but these weren't normal circumstances. His private jet was already being fueled up for tomorrow's flight.

He tapped his pen repeatedly on the desk. Why did Clara have to pick now to elope? Not that he wasn't happy for her. He was. He just wasn't happy about the surprise. Okay, so he didn't like surprises and certainly not when they caused his plans to go awry.

Just like his evening with Holly. Talk about everything going sideways—in a mind-blowing way. It'd been weeks since they'd been together and he still couldn't get her out of his system. Though they'd agreed there would be no repeat of the amazing evening, he regretted letting her go more than he thought possible.

* * *

What had she been thinking?

Holly Abrams stood alone in the elevator at Lockwood International. She pressed the button for the top floor—Finn's floor. The last time she'd visited the executive suite things had spiraled totally out of control. One moment they were talking work and the next she'd been in Finn's luxury penthouse. The memory made her stomach dip.

There'd been candles, delicious food, sparkling wine and honeyed compliments. It'd been quite a heady combination. And when at last he'd pressed his lips to hers, she'd have sworn she'd fallen head over heels in love with him. It was though this thing had been building between them since they first met. Love at first sight?

She didn't believe in it. This thing, it had to be infatuation—a great big case of it. And even though they'd mutually agreed to go their separate ways, her oasis at the office had turned stressful with reminders of Finn at every turn.

The elevator dinged and the door slid open. She stepped out. Taking a deep, steadying breath, she started down the hallway toward Clara's desk—toward Finn's office. However, Clara wasn't at her desk. Holly's gaze moved to Finn's closed door. She had a moment of déjà vu and her heart raced.

The door swung open. Who was it? Finn?

And then Clara stepped into the hallway. Holly sighed. She dismissed the disappointment that assailed her as Clara headed toward her.

The young woman's eyes reflected an inner turmoil. "There you are. Thank goodness you came."

"What's the matter?"

"Everything."

"Whoa. It can't be that bad."

"You're right." The frown on Clara's face said otherwise. "I... I need to ask you for a huge favor. And I'll totally understand if you can't do it. I just don't know anyone else who can help. And this just has to work out—"

"Slow down. Tell me what it is." Holly thought of Clara as a friend ever since they met on the charity committee. The woman was always generous in word and deed.

"My boyfriend proposed last night." A smile lifted her lips as she held up her left hand.

"Wow! Congratulations! I'm so happy for you." She gave Clara a brief hug.

Clara pulled back. "Thank you. It really was a surprise. We've been together for over five years now. I'd pretty much given up on him ever proposing. Anyway the plan is we catch a plane tomorrow and elope in Vegas followed by a honeymoon in Napa Valley. I can't postpone it. I don't want him changing his mind."

"Don't worry. Everything will work out." She was happy that Clara was finally getting her happily-ever-after. Holly didn't see such a rosy future for herself, but it didn't mean she didn't believe it could happen for others. "What can I do to help?"

"I know this is a lot to ask, but I need you to fill in for me while I'm off on my honeymoon."

"What?" Clara wanted her to be Finn's assistant? No. Impossible. Finn would never agree. She must have misunderstood. "You want me to be Mr. Lockwood's assistant?"

Clara nodded. "It won't be for long."

Her friend had absolutely no idea what she was asking of her. None whatsoever. She'd given Finn her word that she'd stay clear of him just as he'd agreed to do the same for her.

Now it appeared she had to make a very difficult choice— keep her word to Finn or keep her friendship with Clara. Holly's stomach plummeted into her Louis Vuittons. She desperately wanted to do both.

But that wasn't possible.

CHAPTER TWO

THERE HAD TO be a way out.

But how? Holly couldn't bear to hurt Clara's feelings. But Holly acting as Finn's assistant for even the briefest time would be at the very least awkward. It'd raise too many memories—memories best left alone.

How did she explain that this arrangement would never work? No one knew about that special evening she'd spent with Finn. And it had to remain that way.

Holly smoothed a nonexistent wrinkle from her skirt. "I can't just move up here. What about my work in the legal department?"

Clara sent her a pleading look with her eyes. "If that's all you're worried about, I worked it out with your boss. You are temporarily transferred here. But don't worry. Working for Mr. Lockwood comes with benefits."

She'd already sampled Mr. Lockwood's benefits and they were unforgettable, but she was certain that was not what Clara meant. "Did you talk this over with F...ah, Mr. Lockwood?"

Clara's eyes momentarily widened at Holly's slip of the tongue. "I did and he's on board."

He was? Really? She was running out of excuses about why this wouldn't work. But maybe this was the break she was looking for. If Finn was open to taking her on as his assistant, would it be such a stretch to think he'd consider giving her a personal referral?

It was time she left Lockwood International. And like a sign, there was an opening at another *Fortune 500* company for an assistant to the lead counsel. She'd heard about the position through a friend of a friend. But the attorney was older and wanted someone closer to his age with top qualifications.

The cards were stacked against Holly as she was in her twenties and her experience was so-so, depending on what the position required. But it would be a big boost for her and it would make it possible for her mother to make her time off permanent.

Holly had come up with one thing that just might make gaining the new position a real possibility, a letter of recommendation from Finn—a well-respected businessman. Although she hadn't quite figured out how to approach him. But then again, it appeared he'd taken that problem out of her hands.

After all, she'd only have to be his PA for one week and then he'd be on his annual holiday. She'd have the office to herself. In the meantime, it wasn't like they were going to be working in the same office. He'd be down the hall behind a closed door and she'd be out here. If he could make it work, then so could she.

"I'll do it."

Clara's face lit up like a Christmas tree. "I was hoping you'd say that. I can spend the rest of today going over current projects with you, but first let's go get you introduced to Mr. Lockwood."

On wooden legs, Holly followed Clara down the hallway. Her morning coffee sloshed in her stomach, making her nauseated. *Keep it together. Just act professional.*

Clara knocked on the door and then entered. Holly followed her inside. Her heart picked up its pace as her gaze eagerly sought him out. His hair appeared freshly trimmed. And the blue button-up accentuated his broad, muscular shoulders. Holly swallowed hard.

He glanced up from his computer monitor. Was that surprise reflected in his blue-gray eyes? It couldn't be. He'd approved this scenario. In a blink, the look was gone.

"Mr. Lockwood, I'd like to introduce Holly Abrams." Clara's voice drew Holly from her thoughts. "She's from the legal department."

"We've met." His gaze moved between the two women. "The question is what's she doing in my office?"

Clara sent him a nervous smile. "She's agreed to step up and fill in for me while I'm away on my honeymoon. Her boss in legal gave nothing but rave reviews about her."

"I see." Finn's gaze moved to Holly.

What was she missing here? Hadn't Clara said Finn had approved of this temporary assignment? She forced a smile to her lips as his intense gaze held her captive. Her heart continued to race and her palms grew damp. She should say something, but the jumbled words in her mind refused to form a cohesive sentence.

Clara spoke, breaking the mounting silence. "She'll do a really good job for you."

"I don't know about this." Finn leaned back in the black leather chair. "Why don't you give us a moment to talk?" Clara made a discreet exit. It wasn't until the door snicked shut that Finn spoke again with a serious, no-nonsense tone. "Okay, we're alone now. Please explain to me what happened to our agreement to keep clear of each other."

"Clara said that she okayed this with you. I figured if you were big enough to deal with this awkward situation for Clara's sake then so was I. After all, Clara would do most anything for anyone. And it is her wedding—"

"Enough. I get the point. But this—" he gestured back and forth between them "—it won't work."

"That's fine with me. Do you have someone else who can fill in?"

Finn cleared his throat. "No, I don't."

Holly clasped her hands together to keep from fidgeting and straightened her shoulders. "I know that we've never worked together, but I think I can do the job."

Finn leaned back in his chair and crossed his arms. "Tell me why I should give you a chance."

Holly swallowed hard, not expecting to have to interview for the position, but when she recalled the desperation in her friend's voice, she knew she couldn't let Clara down. "I'm a hard worker. I'm the first through the door in the morning and I'm the last out in the evening."

"Are you sure that's a good thing? Perhaps you just don't get your work done in a timely manner."

Her gaze narrowed. Why exactly was he giving her such a hard time? A smart retort teetered on the tip of her tongue, but she choked it back, refusing to let him provoke her. "No. I like to be punctual. I like to have the coffee brewing and a chance to take off my coat before the phone starts ringing. And I don't rush out the door at the end of the day simply because I can't. I usually have a task or two dropped on my desk by my boss as he's leaving."

Finn nodded as though her answer pleased him. "And you think you're up to the challenges of being my PA?"

"I do."

"You do realize that what happened between us is in the past. It will have no bearing on our working relationship."

"I wouldn't have it any other way."

"Good."

"Does that mean I have the position?" The breath caught in her throat as she waited for his answer.

Seconds ticked by and still he said nothing. What in the world? She thought of all the things she could say to him to sell herself, but she didn't want to look desperate because she wasn't. Oh, maybe she was just a bit. She had a plan and he played a pivotal role.

"Okay. You've convinced me. We'll do this."

The breath rushed from Holly's straining lungs. "Thank you. I'll go catch up on everything I need to know from Clara."

"Holly, remember this is strictly work."

Like she could or would forget. "I understand, Mr. Lockwood."

He frowned. "I don't think we have to be that formal. Finn will do."

"Yes, sir...erm...Finn."

This was it, she was in. She should be inwardly cheering or smiling or something. And yet she stood there transfixed by the man who danced through her dreams each night and left her longing for a glance of him each day. The truth was that she didn't know how to react. It was one of those good news–bad news scenarios.

The best thing she could do was leave. The sooner, the better. She turned for the door.

"Holly, there's one more thing." He waited until she turned around before continuing. "Make sure you aren't late tomorrow morning. Takeoff is at six a.m. sharp."

"Takeoff?"

Finn's brows scrunched together. "Clara didn't tell you?"

"Tell me what?"

"We're leaving first thing in the morning for the Caribbean. I have an extremely important meeting there."

This was not what she'd been expecting at all. How was she supposed to fly to a sunny destination spot with the sexiest guy alive—a man who could heat her blood with just a look? She inwardly groaned. She was in so much trouble here.

Not only was she nervous about being around him—about remembering their first night together in vivid detail—but she was also a nervous flier, as in white-knuckling it through turbulence. Exactly how long was a flight from New York City to the Caribbean?

No matter what, she wasn't about to back out of this arrangement. There was too much riding on it—too many people counting on her. Her mother's pale face flashed in her mind. After her mother's recent stroke, the doctor had warned that with her other medical conditions, if she didn't slow down, her health would be put at greater risk. Holly needed to do whatever she could to further her career in order to support her and her mother.

"Holly? Will that be a problem?"

His voice drew her from her frantic thoughts. "I didn't know. Where will we be staying?"

"On my private island."

Oh, boy! One private island. One sexy guy. And a whole lot of chemistry. What could possibly go wrong with this scenario?

CHAPTER THREE

TWENTY-TWO MINUTES LATE, Holly rushed through the airport early the next morning. Her suitcase *clunk-clunked* as it rolled over the tiled floor.

She hadn't meant to stay up late the night before, talking on the phone, but it'd been a long time since she'd heard her mother so exuberant. Apparently the Sunshine State agreed with her, especially the strolls along the beach while Holly's aunt was off at her waitressing job.

When her mother mentioned returning to New York, Holly readily assured her there was no rush. At the same time, she'd made a mental note to send her aunt some more money to cover her mother's living expenses. Holly proceeded to fill her mother in on the business trip, citing her absence as another reason for her mother to remain in Florida. Her mother actually sounded relieved, confirming Holly's belief that she needed to do everything to ensure her mother didn't have to worry about money. And that hinged on impressing Finn.

But this morning, if anything could have gone wrong, it had. As late as she was, Finn would think she was incompetent or worse that she'd changed her mind and backed out without a word. And because she'd been so rattled yesterday, she'd forgotten to get his cell number.

When she finally reached the prearranged meeting spot, Finn stood there, frowning. She was breathless and feeling totally out of sorts.

His piercing gaze met hers. "I didn't think you were going to show up."

She attempted to catch her breath. "There was an accident."

Immediately his anger morphed into concern. "Are you okay?"

"It wasn't me. It was the vehicle two cars up from my cab." In that moment the horrific events played in her mind. "One second we're moving along the highway and the next a little sports car attempts to cut off a souped-up pickup truck with large knobby tires. The car swerved wildly across the lanes as tires screeched and the driver tried to regain control, but the car lifted and flipped a couple of times." Tears welled up in her eyes. "I never witnessed something so horrific. I... I don't think the driver made it."

Finn reached out to her and pulled her close. Her cheek rested against his shoulder. "Thank God you're safe."

Her emotions bubbled to the surface. The worry. The fear. The shock. She wasn't sure how much time had passed as Finn continued to hold her. Horrific scenes of the accident played in her mind, one after the other. She knew she shouldn't seek comfort in his arms. Although it was innocent enough, it wasn't part of their agreement. And yet, she didn't move.

It was only when she started to gather herself that she noticed the spicy scent of his cologne. It would be so easy to forget about their agreement and turn in his arms, claiming his very kissable lips. Every cell in her body longed to do just that. Just once more.

But she couldn't. Once would not be enough. Frustration balled up inside her. Besides, he was just being nice—a gentleman. She refused to throw herself at him and ruin everything. After all, she was out to prove to him that she was an invaluable asset in the office.

With great regret, she extricated herself from his arms, already missing the warmth of his touch. "I must be such a mess." She swiped her hands over her cheeks. "Sorry about that. I... I'm usually—"

"No apologies necessary." He waved away her words. "I'm just relieved you're safe."

The sincerity in his words had her glancing up at him. In that moment he'd reverted back to Finn Lockwood, the friendly man who'd taken her to his penthouse to thank her for her help with the contract. The man who'd spent the evening wining and dining her with some pasta he'd whipped up himself. The same man who'd entertained her with tales of hilarious fiascos at the office. The man who'd swept her off her feet.

"What are you thinking?"

His voice drew her from her thoughts. Not about to tell him the truth, she said, "That we should get moving. I've already put you behind schedule."

"You're right." He gestured for her to walk ahead of him.

Her insides shivered with nervous tension. She couldn't tell if it was from being held in Finn's arms or the thought of soaring through the air in his jet. Maybe she should mention her fear of flying to Finn. Then again, they'd already shared more than enough for now. She would just lose herself in her work. If all went well, he'd never even know of her phobia of heights.

What had he been thinking?

Finn sat across the aisle from Holly on his private jet. They were in midflight and Holly had been surprisingly quiet. It suited him just fine. He was preparing for his upcoming meeting, or he had been until thoughts of Holly infiltrated his mind. Truth be told, he hadn't been able to let go of the memories of their night together. She was amazing and so easy to be with. Most people wouldn't find that to be a problem, but he did.

He refused to let someone get close to him—he would do nothing but lead them to unhappiness. Because that was what happened to the people he cared about—he let them down. And Holly was too nice to get caught up with the likes of him.

The onboard phone buzzed. Finn took the call from the pilot. After a brief conversation, he turned to Holly, who had her window shade drawn. He presumed it was to cut down on the glare on her digital tablet. He, on the other hand, enjoyed being able to look out at the world around them. However, the overcast day hampered much of his view. "That was the captain. He said we should buckle our seat belts as we're about to hit some rough weather."

Without argument or for that matter a word, Holly did as he asked. She then returned her attention to the tablet as though she hadn't heard him. What in the world had her so absorbed?

He gave a shake of his head and turned back to his laptop. He'd been working on an agenda for his upcoming meeting, but he'd totally lost track of his line of thought. He started reading the last couple of bullet points when his attention meandered back to Holly.

Giving up on his attempt to work, Finn closed his laptop. He glanced over at her, which was a mistake. He was immediately drawn in by her natural beauty. He loved that she didn't wear heavy makeup, only a little bit to accent her own unique qualities.

There was just something so different about Holly, but he couldn't quite put his finger on exactly what made her so much more appealing than the other women who had passed through his life. Maybe it was that she was content with her life—not looking to him for a leg up in her career. Or maybe it was that she treated him like everybody else instead of trying to cater to him. Whatever it was, he was intrigued by her.

Realizing he was staring, he cleared his throat. "What are you reading?"

She glanced up as though completely lost in thought. "What did you say?"

He smiled, liking the sheepish look on her face and the touch of pink in her cheeks. "I was wondering what had you so deep in thought."

She glanced down at her tablet and then back at him. "Um, nothing."

"Must be something to have you so preoccupied."

"Just some work."

"Work? I don't recall giving you anything to do on the way to the island."

She worried her bottom lip. "I was doing a little research."

"Do tell. I'm thoroughly intrigued."

She set aside her tablet. "I downloaded some background on the businessmen that you'll be meeting with."

"Really? I thought you'd prefer to read a book."

"I like to be prepared. Clara gave me their names. I hope you don't mind."

"What else did she tell you about the meeting?"

"Nothing except that it is extremely important and top secret."

He smiled, liking that Clara had emphasized discretion. Of course, Holly would learn all about his plans soon enough. "Let me know if you uncover anything noteworthy."

"I will." She once more picked up her tablet.

Why was she working so hard on this? Surely she wasn't this thorough normally. There had to be something driving her. Was she afraid of disappointing him?

Or more likely, she was doing whatever she could to ignore him.

Just then the plane started to vibrate. Finn glanced over at Holly and noticed that she had the armrests in a death grip. "Don't worry. It's just some turbulence."

She looked at him, her eyes as big as saucers. "Maybe we should land until it passes over."

"You don't fly much, do you?"

She shook her head. "Never had much reason. Anyplace I've ever wanted to go I can get to by train or car."

"Well, relax. Turbulence is common. It's nothing to worry about."

"Easy for you to say," she said in a huff.

He suppressed a chuckle. She did have spirit. Maybe that was what he liked so much about her. Otherwise, why would he have agreed to this completely unorthodox arrangement?

Perhaps if he could get her talking, she'd temporarily forget about the turbulence. "Where are these places you visit by car or train?"

She glanced at him with an *Are you serious*? look. He continued staring at her, prompting her to talk.

"I… I don't go away often."

"But when you do travel, where do you go?"

"The ocean."

It wasn't much, but it was a start. "Which beach is your favorite?"

"Ocean City and…" The plane shook again. Her fingers tightened on the armrests. Her knuckles were white.

"I must admit I've never been to Ocean City. Is there much to do there?" When she didn't respond, he said, "Holly?"

"Um, yes. Ah, there's plenty to do along the boardwalk. But I like to take a book and sit on the beach."

"What do you read?"

"Mysteries. Some thrillers."

He continued talking books and authors with her. He found that she was truly passionate about books. As she talked about a series of suspense novels she was in the process of reading, his attention was drawn to her lips—her tempting lips. It'd be so easy to forget the reason for this trip and the fact she was helping him out.

What would she say if he were to take her in his arms and press his lips to hers?

His phone buzzed again. After a brief conversation with the pilot, he turned to Holly. "The pilot believes we're past the bad weather. You can relax. It should be smooth flying from here on out."

The tension visibly drained from her as her shoulders relaxed and her hands released the armrests. "That's good news. I guess I'm not a very good flyer."

"Oh, trust me, you're doing fine. I've experienced worse. Much worse." He inwardly shuddered, recalling a couple of experiences while flying commercial airlines.

His attention returned to his laptop. He was surprised the break had him feeling refreshed. His fingers flew over the keyboard. Some time had passed when he grew thirsty.

He got up from his seat. "Can I get you something to drink?"

"That sounds good. But I can get it."

She stood up and followed him to the front of the plane where there was a small kitchenette. "I'm surprised you don't have any staff on board."

"Staff? For just me?" He shook his head. "I don't need anyone standing around, waiting for something to do. Besides, I appreciate the time alone."

"Oh."

"Sorry. I didn't mean that the way it sounded. I'm happy having you along."

"You are?" Her eyes widened. And was that a smile playing at the corners of her lips?

"I am. You're doing me a big favor. This meeting can't be rescheduled. It's time sensitive. And I didn't want to ruin Clara's wedding."

"Seems it all worked out."

He arched a brow. "Did it? Are you really okay with being here?"

"I—"

The plane violently shuddered. Then the plane dipped. A gasp tore from Holly's lips. Her body swayed forward. He sprang into action, catching her.

"It'll be okay."

The fear in her eyes said she didn't believe him.

As the pilot guided the plane through a particularly rough patch of airspace, Finn held on to Holly, who in turn held on to him. This was the exact thing he'd told himself that wouldn't occur on this trip, but fate seemed to have other plans.

He looked down at her as she lifted her chin. Their gazes met and held. Even when the plane leveled out, he continued to hold her. The emotions reflected in her eyes were intense. Or was he reading what he wanted to see in them?

He did know one thing—having her this close was doing all sorts of crazy things to his body. He caught a whiff of her soft floral scent and inhaled deeper. The pleasing scent swept him back to that not-so-long-ago night. Maybe playing it safe was overrated.

The plane started to vibrate again. Her wide-eyed gaze reflected fear. He knew how to distract her. His head dipped. His lips swooped in, claiming hers. She didn't move at first as though surprised by his actions. But in seconds her lips moved beneath his.

Holly was amazing. He'd never met a woman who intrigued him both mentally and physically. Her lips parted and his tongue slipped inside. She tasted of mint with a hint of chocolate. A moan swelled in his throat.

His thoughts turned toward the big bed in the back of the plane. Should he even entertain such an idea? But with the heat of their kiss, it wasn't out of bounds. All he had to do was scoop her up in his arms. It wasn't like it'd be their first time. Or even their second.

There was a sound. But he brushed it off, not wanting

anything to ruin this moment. And yet there it was again. He concentrated for a second and realized it was the private line from the cockpit.

With great regret, he pulled back. "I better get that. It's the pilot."

Her lips were rosy and slightly swollen. And her eyes were slightly dilated. He'd never seen a more tempting sight. And yet his mind told him the interruption was exactly what they needed. It would give them time to come to their senses.

CHAPTER FOUR

"THIS IS YOUR PLACE?"

Holly exited the helicopter that had transported them from the airstrip on the big island to Finn's private island. The landing zone sat atop a hill. It was the only place on the small island cleared of greenery except for the white sandy beach.

Finn moved to her side. "Do you like it?"

"I do. I've only ever seen places like this on television or on the internet. I never imagined I would one day step foot in paradise."

"Paradise?"

"Yes. You don't think so?"

"I never really thought about it." He rolled her suitcase to the edge of the helipad. "I'm afraid we have to walk to the house. It isn't far."

"No worries. This jaunt is nothing compared to the hour I spend each day at the gym sweating my butt off." She pressed her lips together, realizing she'd probably shared more than he ever wanted to know about her.

When she reached for her suitcase, their fingers brushed. He looked at her. "I can take it."

She wasn't about to be treated like a helpless woman. She'd been standing on her own two feet since she was ten and her father had walked out on her and her mother. Someone had to pick up the slack. At that point in time, her mother hadn't been in any condition.

Holly's grip tightened around the handle. "I can manage."

"You do know it'll have to be carried over the rough terrain."

"Understood. I'll count it as exercise on my calorie counter."

He shook his head as he stepped back. "By the way,

there's a gym at the house. Please feel free to use it. I certainly don't make it there nearly enough."

"Thanks. I just might take you up on the offer." When he gestured for her to go ahead of him, she said, "I'd rather follow while I get my bearings."

With a shrug, he set off down the stone path surrounded by lush green foliage.

Her gaze followed him and he set a steady pace.

But it wasn't the beautiful setting that held her attention—it was Finn. His shoulders were broad and muscled, while his waist was trim without an ounce of flub. And his backside, well, it was toned. A perfect package.

"See anything in particular you like?"

Heat rushed to her cheeks. Had he just busted her checking him out? Her gaze lifted and she was relieved to see that he was still facing straight ahead. "Lots. You're so lucky to live here."

"Only part-time. When you're done working, please feel free to use all of the facilities including the pool."

He didn't have to give her any more encouragement. She had every intention of checking it all out since she would never be back here again. "I do have to admit that this does feel strange."

"How so?"

"Leaving the snow and Christmas decorations in New York and landing here where there's nothing but a warm breeze and sunshine. Do you decorate a palm tree instead of a pine tree for Christmas?"

He stopped walking and turned to her. "I don't do either. I thought Clara might have mentioned it."

"She didn't say a word."

"Long story short, I don't like Christmas." He turned and continued along the path to the house.

He didn't like Christmas? She really wanted to hear the long version of that story. Was he a real-life Grinch? Im-

possible. He was friendly—when he wanted to be. Social—
again, when he wanted to be. So why did he hate Christmas?

Wait. Who hated Christmas? It was full of heartwarming, sentimental moments. Twinkle lights. Snowflakes. Presents. Shopping. Definitely lots of shopping. And the most
delicious food.

Whatever. His reasons for not enjoying the holiday were
his problem. They were certainly none of her business. But
that wasn't enough to suppress her curiosity.

"Why don't you like Christmas?" she blurted out.

He stopped. His shoulders straightened. When he turned,
his forehead was creased with lines and his brows were
drawn together. "Does everyone have to enjoy the holidays?"

She shrugged. "I suppose not. But I'm sure they all have
a reason. I was just curious about yours."

"And if I don't want to share?"

"It's your right. I just thought after we talked on the plane
that we were at the stage where we shared things with each
other."

"You mean you equate our talk of books to digging into
my life and finding out how my mind ticks? No." He shook
his head. "My personal life is off limits." His tone lacked its
earlier warmness. In fact, it was distinctly cold and rumbled
with agitation. "You might research prospective business
associates, but I'd appreciate it if you wouldn't put my life
under your microscope."

What is he afraid I'll find?

She gave herself a mental shake. He was right. She was
treading on a subject that was none of her business. His dislike of Christmas had nothing to do with her presence on—
what was the name of this island? She scanned her mind,
but she didn't recall him ever mentioning it.

"What did you say the name of this island is?"

"I didn't."

Surely this wasn't another one of those subjects that was off limits. Even she couldn't be that unlucky.

As though reading her mind, he said, "It's called Lockwood Isle."

Not exactly original, but fitting. "Your own island nation."

He shrugged. "Something like that. It's a place to get away from everything."

Her phone buzzed with a new email. "Not exactly everything. I see there's internet access."

"As much as I'd like to totally escape, I do have an international company to run. I can't cut myself off completely."

Holly was relieved to know that she could keep in contact with her mother. Even though she'd made financial arrangements with her aunt for her mother to make her very first visit to Florida, she still wanted to talk with her daily. Holly needed the reassurance that there weren't any setbacks with her health.

Her gaze strayed back to her host. She might not have to worry too much about her mother right now, but she did have to worry about Finn. That kiss on the plane, it couldn't happen again. He wasn't looking for anything serious and neither was she. Her focus had to be on getting his recommendation for the new job.

Finn stopped walking. "Here we are."

She glanced up at the white house with aqua shutters. The home was raised up on what looked like stilts. Each post was thick like an enormous tree trunk. It certainly looked sturdy enough.

Still staring at the impressive structure, she asked, "Why is the house on pylons? Are there a lot of storms?"

"No. But some of them bring in a high storm surge. I like to be prepared."

She had a feeling it wasn't just storms he liked to be prepared for. He struck her as the type of man who carefully plotted out not only his business but also his whole life, avoiding as many storms as possible.

"Will this do?"

Later that afternoon Finn glanced up from his desk in his study to find Holly standing there in a white sundress, holding a file folder. The bodice hugged her generous curves and tied around her neck, leaving just enough of her cleavage to tempt and tease. He swallowed hard. He should tell her to change clothes because there was no way he could conduct business with her looking so desirable.

Instead, he said, "Thank you." He accepted the file. "By the way, don't forget to pack lots of sunscreen."

"Pack? I never unpacked." Her eyes filled with confusion. "We're leaving?"

"Yes. Tomorrow morning we're setting sail on my yacht."

"Yacht?"

"Did I forget to mention it?" When she nodded, he added, "We'll be cruising around the islands for a couple of days until my business is concluded."

"Sounds great." Her voice lacked conviction.

"Have you been sailing before?"

She hesitated. "No."

Why exactly had he brought her along on this trip? Oh, yes, because her credentials were excellent. But that was when she was in a skyscraper in New York City. She didn't seem to fare so well outside her element. But it was too late to change course now. He just had to hope for the best—definitely not his idea of a good strategy, but the only one he had at this particular moment.

"Don't worry." He hoped to ease the worry lines now marring her face. "The yacht is spacious. You'll have your own stateroom." He took a moment to clarify the importance of the meeting. "I have worked for a number of months to bring these very influential men together. Discretion is of the utmost importance."

She nodded. "I understand. I've worked in your legal department for the past five years. Everything that passed over my desk was confidential. You can count on me."

He knew that. It was one of the reasons he'd agreed to this arrangement. Now, if he could just keep his mind from straying back to her luscious lips. His gaze zeroed in on them. They were painted up in a deep wine color. It was different from her usual earthy tones. But it was a good look on her.

He forced his mind back to business. "Did you reply to all of the outstanding emails?"

"I just finished them. The personal ones I've forwarded to your account as directed. I thought you might have some last-minute items you need completed before the meeting."

She was good. Really good. Normally that would be awesome, but when he was trying to keep her busy to avoid temptation, he wished she wasn't quite so competent.

"Have you returned all of the phone calls?"

She nodded. "I even called my mother."

"Your mother?"

"I just wanted to let her know that we arrived safely. She's actually off on her own holiday."

Was Holly attempting to make small talk? Boy, was he out of practice. He wasn't even sure how to respond. "That's good." He was better off sticking to business. "It sounds like you have everything under control. You can take the rest of the day off. We'll head out this evening as soon as all of our guests have arrived. Why don't you take a book and relax by the pool until then."

"I didn't bring a book. I didn't see a need since I planned to be working."

"But not from the time you woke up until you went to bed."

"You mean like you're doing?"

He glanced down at the papers littering his desk. "Guilty

as charged. But you don't want to end up like me. You're young and have so much to look forward to."

"You make it sound like you're old and your life is almost over."

"My life is Lockwood International. It's the reason I get out of bed in the morning."

"I'm sorry."

"Sorry? Sorry for what?"

"That you think that's all you have to live for."

"It's the way it has to be."

The pity reflected in her eyes had him recoiling. He didn't deserve pity or sympathy. She had no idea about his life— none whatsoever. Not even the press knew the entire truth.

Living and breathing everything about Lockwood International was his punishment. He'd lived while the rest of his family had perished. It was what his aunt had told him quite frequently when he rebelled about doing his schoolwork or having to stay in boarding schools. She told him he had no room to complain. He had lived while the others had died a painful death, and then she'd glare at him like it was all his fault. And for the most part, she was right.

Holly moved to the window. "Have you looked around this place? It's amazing. When's the last time you enjoyed it?"

"I don't have time for fun."

"Everyone needs to loosen up now and then. You don't want your guests showing up and finding that scowl on your face, do you?"

What scowl? He resisted the urge to run his hands over his face.

"I don't scowl." Her eyes widened at the grouchy tone of his voice. What was it about this woman that got under his skin? "I just need to stay on track and focus."

"Then I won't distract you any longer." She turned to the door.

She'd only tried to get him to relax, and yet he'd made her feel awkward. "Holly, wait." When she hesitated, he added, "I've been working so hard to pretend nothing happened between us that I've made matters worse. That was never my intention."

She turned. "Is it that hard to forget?"

"You know it is." His mind spiraled back to the kiss they'd shared on the plane. "But we can't go back there. It was a mistake the first time. And now that the fate of this project rests on how well you and I work together, we can't get distracted."

"I understand. I'll let you get back to work."

After Holly was gone, his concentration was severely lacking. He kept going over their conversation. Was his mood really that transparent? Usually business provided him solace from all that he'd done wrong in life and all that his life was lacking, but he couldn't find that escape anymore. He wondered if he'd done things differently, how his life would have turned out.

His chair scraped over the floor as he got to his feet. There was no point in staring blindly at the monitor. He wasn't going to get any more work done—at least not now. Maybe Holly was right. He should take a break. A run along the beach would be nice.

After changing his clothes, Finn stepped onto the patio. The splash of water drew his attention. He came to a complete halt as he watched Holly swim the length of the pool. He'd had no idea that she had taken him up on his suggestion that she go for a swim. He quietly watched, impressed with the ease of her strokes as she crossed the pool.

If he was smart, he'd head back inside before she noticed him. But his feet wouldn't cooperate. Sometimes being smart was overrated.

When she reached the edge of the pool, she stopped and

straightened. That was when he noticed her barely there turquoise bikini. The breath caught in his throat.

"Oh, hi." Droplets of water shimmered on her body as she smiled up at him. "Did you change your mind about unwinding?"

He struggled to keep his gaze on her face instead of admiring the way her swimsuit accented her curves. He made a point now of meeting her gaze. "I was going to take a run on the beach."

"In this heat?" When he shrugged, she added, "You'd be better off waiting until later when it cools down."

She was right, but he couldn't bring himself to admit it. "I'll be fine."

"Why don't you come swimming instead? The water is perfect."

He moved to the edge of the pool and crouched down. He dipped his hand in the water. She was right. The water was not too cold and not too warm. "I don't want to bother you."

"You won't be. The pool is plenty big for the both of us."

He had his doubts about the pool being big enough for him to keep his hands to himself. And with Holly in that swimsuit, he'd be so tempted to forget that they'd come to the island to work.

Finn raked his fingers through his hair. "I don't know. I really should be working."

"Your problem is that you think about work too much."

And then without warning, she swiped her arm along the top of the water, sending a small wave in his direction. By the time he figured out what she was up to, he was doused in water.

"Hey!" He stood upright and swiped the water from his face. "What was that all about?"

Her eyes twinkled with mischievousness. "Now you don't have an excuse not to join me."

Why was he letting his worries get the best of him and

missing out on this rare opportunity to have some fun? After all, it was just a swim.

"Okay. You win." He stripped off his T-shirt and tossed it on one of the lounge chairs.

He dove into the pool, enjoying the feel of the cool water against his heated body. He swam the length of the pool before returning to Holly. She was still smiling as she floated in the water.

"Not too bad for an old man—"

"Old man. I'll show you who's old. Let's race."

She eyed him up but didn't say a word.

"What's the matter?" he asked. "Afraid of the challenge."

"No. I'm just wondering if an old man like you can keep up with me."

"Seriously? You have to race me now."

She flashed him a teasing grin. "First one back gets their wish."

Without waiting for him, she took off. He smiled and shook his head. And then he set off in her wake. His muscles knew the motions by heart. He'd swam this pool countless times over the years, but this time was different. This time he wasn't alone.

He pushed himself harder. He reached the end of the pool and turned. He wanted to win. Not because he wanted to be the best. And not because he couldn't be a good loser. No. He wanted to win because the winner could name their wish.

And his wish—

His hand struck the end of the pool. His head bobbed above the water. A second later Holly joined him.

"About time you got here," he teased.

She sent him a cheesy grin before sending another splash of water in his direction. He backed away, avoiding most of the spray.

Holly was about to swim away when he said, "Not so fast. I won."

"And?"

"And I get my wish." He moved closer to her.

She didn't back away. It was as though she knew what he wanted. Was he that obvious?

Her voice grew softer. "And what did you have in mind?"

His gaze dipped to her lips. It seemed like forever since he last felt her kiss. There was something about her that got into his veins and made him crave her with every fiber of his being.

His gaze rose and met hers. His heart hammered against his ribs. Was she as turned on as he was? There was only one way to find out.

He reached out to her. Her skin was covered with goose bumps. He knew how to warm her up. His fingers slid over her narrow waist.

He'd never wanted anyone as much as Holly. And she was the last person he should desire. She was a serious kind of girl—the kind who didn't get around.

She was the type of woman you married.

The thought struck him like a lightning rod. As though she'd also had a moment of clarity, they both pulled back. Talk about an awkward moment.

"I...ah, should get back to work." Holly headed for the pool steps.

It was best that he didn't follow her, not right now. "I'll be in shortly. I think I'll swim a few more laps."

Finn groaned before setting off beneath the cool water, hoping to work Holly out of his system. He was beginning to wonder if that was even possible. He kicked harder and faster.

The one thing he knew was that he wasn't falling for Holly. No way. He didn't have room in his life for that major complication.

CHAPTER FIVE

ONE POUNDING HEART pressed to the other. Heated gazes locked. Lips a breath apart.

Holly gave herself a mental jerk. Not even a night's sleep had lessened the intensity of that moment in the pool with Finn. Oh, how she'd wanted to feel his touch again.

But then she'd spotted the passion in his eyes. One kiss wouldn't have been enough—for either of them. The acknowledgment of just how deep this attraction ran had startled her. She'd pulled back at the same time as Finn.

Now aboard Finn's luxury yacht, the *Rose Marie*, Holly took a seat off to the side of the room as the meeting commenced. With a handful of notable and influential businessmen in attendance, she couldn't let herself dwell on the almost-kiss. As each man took a seat at the long teakwood table, she quietly observed. Her job was to step in only when needed. Other than that, she was to remain virtually invisible on the sidelines.

So this is the hush-hush, wink-wink meeting.

A small smile pulled at Holly's lips as she glanced around the room. Finn sat at the head of the table in a white polo shirt and khaki shorts. A very different appearance from what she was accustomed to seeing on those rare times when she caught a glimpse of him at the office.

On either side of the table sat four men. Mr. Wallace, Mr. Santos, Mr. McMurray and Mr. Caruso. All influential men in their own rights—from toys to office supplies, electronics and snack foods. No wonder there were bodyguards littering the upper deck.

"Welcome." Finn began the meeting. "I've invited you all here in hopes that we will be able to rescue Project Santa."

He'd given her the information about this holiday project just before the meeting. He made it perfectly clear that it was not to be leaked to anyone for any reason. What took place on this boat was to remain top secret for now.

Talk about surprised.

Holly stared at Finn as though seeing him for the first time. He was a man known for his shrewd business dealings, not his philanthropy. And here she thought this meeting was about conquering the world—about a major corporate take-over. She couldn't have been more wrong.

Finn and his cohorts were planning a way to bring Christmas to many underprivileged children. If it worked, it would be the beginning of an ongoing project aimed at putting food and educational materials in the hands of children.

Holly was truly in awe of Finn. He was such a contra-diction at times. He worked long, hard hours, but he didn't expect his employees to do the same. He didn't celebrate Christmas, yet he planned Project Santa. At the office, he was all about profits and yet here he was planning to donate a portion of those profits to people in need.

For a man who hated Christmas, he certainly was doing a fine job of filling the boots of Santa this year. And she was more than willing to help him pull off this Christmas miracle. Although it was odd to have all of this talk about Christmas and presents surrounded by sunshine and the blue waters of the Caribbean.

Holly redirected her attention to the meeting, taking notes on her laptop and pulling up information as needed. She was tasked with running interference when tempers soared. Each of these men were billionaires and used to getting their own way, so compromise was not something they en-tertained often.

Some wanted to switch the Project Santa packaging to gift bags to cut costs. Others wanted to make the content more meaningful—something that wouldn't just entertain but help the recipient.

"Gentlemen." Finn's face was creased with stress lines. "This was all decided long ago. It's too late to change our plans. The gift boxes are strategically packed according to the location of each child."

Mr. McMurray leaned forward. "And how do we know these packages will get to the children?"

"Yeah, I've heard that a lot of these outreach programs are fronts for scams." Mr. Caruso, a gray-haired man, crossed his arms. "What if they steal them?"

"I hear your concerns. That's why some of my best Lockwood employees will escort each shipment to their destination. They are each tasked with making sure the packages get to their intended targets."

There was a murmur of voices. Holly noticed that Finn wasn't happy with the distractions, but he patiently let the men voice their concerns before they moved on to the reason for this meeting.

"Gentlemen, we need to address the problem we have with the lack of transportation now that Fred has suddenly pulled out."

Thanks to her research, Holly knew Fred Silver owned a delivery company that spanned the globe. As she listened to the men, she learned a federal raid on a number of Fred's distribution centers put his whole company in peril. It seemed Fred didn't have enough controls in place and the cartel got a foothold in his distribution routes. What a mess.

"Without Fred, I don't see how it's possible to complete Project Santa." Mr. Wallace shook his bald head in defeat.

"I agree." Mr. McMurray leaned back in his chair. "It's already December. It's too late to fix this."

The other men nodded in agreement.

Mr. Caruso stared at Finn. "But we still have all of the

books, toys and whatnot already allocated to this project. What do we do with it all?"

The men started talking at once. Voices were raised as each tried to talk over the other. Holly found it amusing that these men, who were well-respected in their own worlds, had a tough time playing nice with their peers. Each thought they had the right answer. And none wanted to stop and consider the other's perspective.

"Gentlemen!" Finn leaned forward, resting his elbows on the table. A hush fell over the room. "I think we need some coffee."

Finn glanced at Holly, prompting her into motion. She moved to grab the coffeepot with one hand and in the other she picked up a tray of pastries. As she headed for the table, each man settled back in their chair as though gathering their thoughts.

Holly pasted on her best and brightest smile. "Mr. Wallace, can I get you some coffee?"

The deep-set frown melted from the man's face and in its place was the beginning of a smile. "Why, yes, coffee sounds good."

She turned the coffee cup upright on the saucer and started to fill it. "I think what you all have come together to do is amazing. Project Santa will give hope to so many children." And then she had an idea. "And it will be such great publicity for your companies."

"Publicity." Mr. Wallace shook his head. "There's to be no publicity. Is that what Finn told you?"

"No, he didn't. I just presumed—obviously incorrectly." She was utterly confused. She'd missed something along the way. "Why then are all of you working so hard on this project when you each have global companies to tend to?"

They leaned back in their chairs as though contemplating her question. That was exactly what she was hoping would happen—that they'd remember why they were here and not give up. In the meantime, she served coffee for everyone.

"Finn should have told you." Mr. Santos reached for the creamer in the center of the table. "We each have so much that we wanted to do something to help those who have had a rough start in life. And with this being the season of giving, Finn came up with this idea. If we can make it work, it might be the beginning of something bigger."

"That sounds fantastic." Holly smiled, hoping to project her enthusiasm. "Too bad you can't make it work—you know, now that Mr. Silver isn't able to participate. I'm sure it's too big of a problem for you men to work around at this late date. Those poor children."

She turned to Finn, whose eyes widened. Oh, no. Had she gone too far? She'd merely wanted to remind these powerful men that they'd overcome greater obstacles in order to make their respective companies household names. If they really put their heads together and pulled in their resources, she was certain they could overcome this issue.

"She's right." Finn's voice commanded everyone's attention. "We can't stop now."

Tensions quickly rose as each powerful man became vocal about their approach to overcome these last hurdles and make the project a go. But this time they were pausing to hear each other out. And at times, building on each other's ideas.

Finn mouthed, "Thank you."

It wasn't exactly the use of her mind that she'd prefer, but the more she heard about this project, the more she believed in it—the more she believed in Finn. He was nothing like his ruthless businessman persona that was portrayed by the press. Why didn't he show the world this gentle, caring side of himself?

After spending hours to resolve the transportation problem with Project Santa, they were still no closer than they had been that morning.

Finn had just showered and changed into slacks and a dress shirt before meeting up with his associates for a card game. This trip wasn't all business. He'd learned long ago that keeping his allies happy was just as important as presenting them with a profitable deal.

He'd just stepped out of his cabin and glanced up to find Holly coming toward him. Her hair was wet and combed back. She looked refreshed and very tempting. His gaze dipped, finding she was wearing a white bikini. She must have been unwinding in the hot tub. He swallowed hard. *Look away. Concentrate on her face.*

Finn met her amused gaze. "Thank you."

"For what?" She adjusted a white towel around her slender waist.

His mouth grew dry. "For your help at the meeting. You were a big help getting everyone to work together."

"I'm glad I could help."

And then realizing they were talking in the hallway where anyone might overhear, he opened his cabin door. "But the distribution is more than we can overcome at this late date."

Holly didn't move. "Actually, I have some thoughts about your problem with the distribution. I don't think it's insurmountable."

He worried that she was a bit too confident. This was a national endeavor—coast to coast. But he had to admit he was intrigued. "Why don't you step in here a moment?"

Her hesitant gaze moved from him to the interior of his stateroom and then back to him. "I really shouldn't. I'm still wet."

"I promise I won't keep you for long. In fact, I'm due at a card game in a couple of minutes."

She noticeably relaxed. Without another word, she passed by him and entered the room. His heart thumped as he contemplated reaching out and pulling her close. What was it about her that had such a hold over him?

She turned as he pushed the door closed. She averted her gaze as her hands wrung together. Was she aware of the energy arching between them? Could she feel his draw to her? Was she as uncertain as he was about what to do about it?

"I don't think I told you, but your boat is amazing." She looked everywhere but at him. "I had no idea they were so elaborate."

"I'm glad you like your accommodations. I take it you enjoy sailing more than you do flying?"

"Definitely. I don't have to worry about falling out of the sky and—"

"No, you don't," he said, not wanting her to finish that graphic image. "If there's anything you want but can't find, just let me know."

"You know if you keep this up, you'll ruin your image."

"My image?"

At last, her gaze met his. "The one of you being a heartless corporate raider."

He pressed a hand to his chest. "I'm wounded. Do you really believe those nasty rumors?"

"Not anymore. I've seen the part you hide from the outside world." Her voice took on a sultry tone as her gaze dipped to his mouth. "Why do you do that?"

He swallowed hard, losing track of the conversation. "Do what?"

"Hide behind your villainous persona when in reality you're not like that at all."

His gaze shifted to her rosy lips. "How am I?"

"You're tough and hard on the outside, but inside..." She stepped closer, pressing a hand to his chest. "In there where it matters, you have a big heart."

"No one ever said that before."

Her hand remained on his chest as though branding him as hers and hers alone. "They just don't know you like I do."

His heart pounded against his ribs. "And do you like what you've gotten to know?"

"Most definitely."

His hand covered hers. "You do know if you don't leave right now that I'm not responsible for what happens next."

"But what about your guests?"

"They're involved in a card game."

"Oh, yes, the card game. You don't want to miss it."

By now she had to be able to feel the rapid beating of his heart. "I don't think they'll miss me."

"Are you sure?"

He nodded, not caring if they did. There was nowhere else he wanted to be at this moment. "Are you sure about this? You and me?"

"I'm sure that I want you to kiss me."

"Holly, I'm serious."

"I am, too. You do still want me, don't you?"

He groaned. "You know that I do."

His hands wrapped around her shapely hips and pulled her to him. In the process her towel came undone, pooling at her feet. He continued to stare into her eyes, watching to see if she'd change her mind, but he only found raw desire reflected in them.

She lifted up on her tiptoes and he didn't waste a moment claiming her lips. He was beginning to think he'd never tire of kissing her. The thought should worry him, but right now he had other things on his mind—things that were drowning out any common sense.

As their kiss deepened, so did his desires. Once was definitely not enough with Holly. Her beauty started on the inside and worked its way out. If he were to ever entertain the idea of getting serious with someone, it would be her.

Her fingers slid up his neck and combed through his hair. Her curves leaned into him, causing a moan to form in the back of his throat. Perhaps they could be friends with benefits. There wouldn't be any harm in that, would there?

He clearly recalled when things ended between them that Holly had said she didn't want anything serious. In fact, she was the first one to say there couldn't be anything more between them. For a moment he'd been floored and then relieved.

Now as her lips moved passionately over his, he wondered what he'd been thinking by letting her walk away. They had so much to offer each other with no strings attached.

But first he had to be sure Holly was still on board with the idea. He just couldn't have her expecting some sort of commitment from him because in the end, he'd wind up letting her down.

He grudgingly pulled back. Cupping her face in his hands, he gazed deep into her eyes. "Holly, are you sure about this?"

She nodded.

"Even though it'll never lead to anything serious?"

Again she nodded. "I told you I don't do serious."

A smile tugged at his lips. How could someone be as perfect as her? The thought got shoved to the back of his mind as she reached up and pulled his head down to meet her lips. This was going to be a night neither of them would forget—

Knock-knock.

"Hey, Finn, you coming?" Mr. Caruso's jovial voice came through the door. "Everyone's anxious to get the game started."

Holly and Finn jumped apart as though they were teenagers having been caught making out beneath the bleachers. She looked at the door and then him. Her lips lifted into a smile before she started to laugh. Finn frowned at her. She pressed a hand to her lips, stifling the stream of giggles.

"I'll be right with you." Finn ran a hand over his mouth,

making sure there were no lingering signs of lip gloss. And then he finger-combed his hair.

Holly gestured that she would wait in the bathroom. He expelled a sigh of relief. He really didn't want to have to explain what she was doing in his room scantily dressed in that tempting bikini.

With Holly out of sight and his clothes straightened, he opened the door. "Sorry I'm running late. I had something come up at the last minute. You know how it is."

The man clapped him on the shoulder. "You work too hard. Come on. The guys are waiting."

"I don't think so. I really need to finish this—"

"Work can wait, your guests can't." Mr. Caruso reached out, grabbed his arm and pulled him into the hallway. "After all, you're the host."

Finn glanced back in his suite longingly, knowing the exquisite night he'd be missing. Playing cards had never looked so dull and tedious before.

"You coming?"

With a sigh, Finn pulled the door shut. "Sure. The work can wait till later."

"Try the morning. I have a feeling this game is going to last most of the night. Should we invite your assistant?"

"I passed her in the hallway earlier. Holly—um, Ms. Abrams called it a night already."

"That's too bad. I like her."

He liked her, too—perhaps far more than was wise. Or perhaps he was blowing everything out of proportion since it'd been a while since he'd been dating. In fact, he hadn't dated anyone since his evening with Holly. No other woman had even tempted him after her. He wasn't sure what to make of that.

CHAPTER SIX

THE NEXT MORNING Holly awoke late. But she didn't feel too guilty. It was work that had her burning the midnight oil—not Finn.

She ran her fingers over her lips, recalling Finn's kiss before he'd left her for the card game. If there hadn't been a knock at his door, she knew where things would have led. Part of her knew it was for the best, but another part ached for the missed opportunity.

What was wrong with her? Why couldn't she be immune to his charms? It was like once his lips touched hers any logic disengaged and her impulses took over. She wondered if he had this effect over all women or just her.

She knew this thing between them couldn't go anywhere. Her experience with men should be proof enough. First, her father walked out on her and her mother. And then while she was earning her paralegal degree, she'd met Josh. He was good-looking and charming. Deciding all men couldn't be like her father, she let herself fall for him.

Holly felt ill as the memories washed over her. Everything between her and Josh had been great for a while. In fact, it was the happiest she'd ever been. And then she'd learned Josh had a gambling problem that led to him stealing from her—the person he was supposed to love. She'd arranged to get him help and he'd sworn he would complete the twelve-step program.

She'd wanted to believe him, but after what her father had done to her mother, Holly had to be sure. And that was when she'd caught Josh in a web of lies with another woman. Holly's stomach soured at the memory.

The depth of his betrayal had cut her deep. After Josh,

she'd sworn off relationships. Her independence gave her a much-needed sense of security. And with her full attention focused on her work, she didn't have time to be lonely. Guys just weren't worth the heartache. And she'd stuck by her pledge until now. Finn had her questioning everything—

Knock-knock-knock.

She had a feeling there'd only be one person who'd come calling at her door this early in the morning. Still, she asked, "Who is it?"

"It's me." The voice was very distinct. "Finn."

"Hang on." She scrambled out of bed and rushed to grab her robe. It was then that she noticed her stomach didn't feel right. It was way more than being upset about the unpleasant memories. She took a calming breath, willing the queasiness away.

She moved to the door and pulled it open. Finn stood there freshly showered and shaved, looking like he was ready to tackle the world. "Good morning."

His gaze narrowed in on her. "Everything okay?"

She ran a hand over her hair. "Sorry. I slept in." Her stomach lurched. She pressed a hand to her midsection, willing it to stop. "I'll, ah, take a quick shower and be right with you."

"You know, you don't look so good."

Right then her stomach totally revolted. She dashed to the bathroom. Thankfully her cabin wasn't that big. She was quite certain she wouldn't have made it another step. She dropped to her knees, sick as a dog. What in the world? She hadn't even eaten that morning.

Once her stomach calmed, she heard the sink turn on. Finn? He was here? He'd witnessed her at her worst. She would have groaned, but she feared doing anything that might upset her stomach again.

"Here. Take this." He handed her a cold cloth.

"You shouldn't be here."

"And leave you alone when you obviously don't feel well?"

No matter what she said, he wasn't leaving. And at that moment she didn't have the energy to argue. Once she'd cleaned up, she walked back to the bedroom. Her stomach wasn't totally right, but it did feel somewhat better.

"I'm sorry about that." Her gaze didn't fully meet his. "You...you were quite the gentleman. Thank you."

"Do you know what's bothering you? Is it something you ate?"

"I think it's seasickness."

"I'm sure it doesn't help that we hit some rough water this morning. Are you sure that's all it is?"

She nodded, certain it had to be the constant roll of the boat.

"You should lie down."

"I don't have time."

"Sure you do." He guided her back to the king-size bed. "Stay here. I'll be right back."

She did as he asked, hoping she'd soon feel like herself. He disappeared out the door like a man on a mission. As she lay there, her mind strayed to her plan for Project Santa. Perhaps she should run it by Finn first. She didn't want to do anything to embarrass either of them in front of those powerful men.

A few minutes later Finn came rushing back into the room. "How are you feeling now?"

"Better." It wasn't a lie.

"I grabbed some ginger ale and toast. Hopefully you'll be able to keep that down. And I grabbed some medicine for the motion sickness."

"Thank you." She sat up in bed and accepted the glass of soda. She tentatively took a sip, not sure what to expect when it hit her stomach. Thankfully, it remained calm.

"I also talked with the captain and he's set course for what he hopes is smoother water."

Finn was changing his trip just for her? She didn't know what to think, except that Finn was a lot more Santa-like than Grinchy.

She took another drink of the soda. So far, so good. Anxious to get on with her day, she got to her feet. She glanced over to find Finn staring at her. "What?"

"The look on your face. Something is bothering you. Is it your stomach again?"

She shook her head. "I told you I'm feeling better."

He sighed. "You're sure? You're not just telling me this to get rid of me?"

"I'm certain. I'll just get showered and be up to the meeting soon."

"I could use your help, but I don't want you pushing yourself." His gaze searched her face and then he moved to the door. "I should be going."

"Finn?"

"Yes."

"There is something I wanted to talk to you about."

His brow arched. "Is it about your health?"

"No. It's nothing like that. It's just an idea I wanted to run past you."

He glanced at his Rolex. "I'd be happy to hear you out, but not right now. I'm late." He opened the door. "I'll see you on deck." He rushed out the door.

"But—"

The door closed. Her words had been cut off. A frown pulled at her lips. She knew how to help him with Project Santa if he'd just slow down and listen to her. She refused to give up now. There had to be a way to get his attention.

Had he made a mistake?

Finn sat uncomfortably at the end of the table, knowing

if they didn't come up with a reasonable resolution to their transportation problem today that they would have to cut their losses and scrap the idea of Project Santa. The thought deeply troubled him.

He glanced at his watch for the third time in ten minutes. Where was Holly? Had she been struck with another bout of sickness?

"Listen, I know we need a solution regarding transportation, but all of my rigs are booked from now until Christmas, delivering our toys to stores." Mr. Wallace tapped his pen on the blank legal pad. "Besides, this wasn't my part of the arrangement. It's not my fault Fred wasn't on top of his business dealings and got in bed with the cartel."

Mr. Caruso sighed. "I couldn't possibly reroute all of my snack food shipments. It'd be a logistic disaster. And it would only cover the east coast. What about the children west of the Mississippi?"

All eyes turned to Mr. Santos. The guy shook his head. "I'm in the same boat. My network is on the east coast. And I have no transportation."

That left one man who hadn't spoken up, Mr. McMurray. He cleared his throat, visibly uncomfortable being in the hot seat. "And what makes you all think I can pull this off when none of you can?"

Immediately everyone spoke at once, defending why they couldn't take over the shipping part of the plan. Finn sat back quietly wondering why he ever thought they'd be able to pull off such a big project. It dashed his hopes for future projects of this scale.

At that moment Holly walked into the room. A hush fell over the men and Finn knew why. She looked like a knockout. She wore an aqua, sleeveless sundress. Her golden-brown hair had been piled on top of her head while corkscrew curls framed her face. She wore a little makeup, but definitely on the conservative side. If he hadn't known that she was feeling under the weather earlier, he wouldn't have been able to guess it by looking at her.

"Good morning, gentlemen. I'm sorry to be late. But I promise I was hard at work."

The tension around the table evaporated, replaced with smiles and warm greetings. Finn shook his head in disbelief. Who'd have thought a bunch of workaholics could be so easily swayed by a pretty face and long, toned legs?

"Don't let me interrupt your discussion." Holly moved to the chair she'd sat in the day before.

Mr. Wallace grunted. "You didn't interrupt much. Everyone was just making excuses about why they couldn't take on the shipping portion of Project Santa. We could use a fresh perspective. Do you have any thoughts on the matter?"

"Actually, I do. First, I want to say I'm very impressed with the endeavor you all are undertaking." She made a point of making eye contact with each man. "And if you would indulge me, I might have a suggestion about the transportation problem."

"Holly." The room grew silent. Finn had to give her a chance to gracefully bow out. "Perhaps I didn't make clear the enormity of this project. The gifts will need to be delivered from coast to coast in every town or city where our companies have a presence."

She nodded as her steady gaze met his. "I understood." She leveled her shoulders. "From what I understand, you have a master list of names and locations for the gifts. You also have all of the items sorted and boxed. All you're lacking is a delivery system."

Finn noticed a couple of the men had started to fidget with their cell phones. They didn't have faith in Holly's ability to overcome such a large obstacle. He had to admit he didn't know what she could do that they hadn't already considered.

"That would be correct." Finn really wanted to know where she was headed. He didn't like surprises. "We have a sorting facility in St. Louis. From there the packages need to be distributed to numerous cities."

"And if I understand correctly, you were planning to do this by way of long-haul trucks."

"Yes, until Fred's company was seized by the government. There's no way he'll be able to unravel that ugly mess in time to help us. So do you have a lead on some other trucking firm?"

She shook her head. "My idea is a little different. I started to think about all of the modes of transport. And then I started to think about who I knew in the transportation industry. And I realized my neighbor in New York is a pilot."

Finn cleared his throat. "So you're suggesting we have your friend fly all of the packages around the country."

She frowned at him. "Of course not. That wouldn't be possible considering there are thousands of packages."

"Then I'm not following what you're telling us."

"My friend is a pilot, but he's just one of many. When he's not flying commercially, he takes part in a national flying club." She glanced around the table and when no one said anything, she explained further. "This flying club has hundreds of members around the country. If we were to enlist their help, we could get the packages to their destinations."

"I don't know." Finn had to think this over. The men started chatting amongst themselves. Finn glanced up to find Holly with a determined look on her face. When she opened her mouth to elaborate, no one noticed.

Finn cleared his throat and then said loudly, "Gentlemen, shall we let Ms. Abrams finish her presentation?"

When silence fell over the room, Holly continued. "I've already put feelers out to see if there would be an interest in helping such a worthy cause, and I have close to a hundred pilots willing to fly the packages."

Finn rubbed his chin. "You trust these people? And they're going to do it out of the goodness of their hearts?"

"Yes, I trust them. And aren't you all doing this project out of the goodness of your hearts?"

One by one the men's heads nodded except Finn's. He didn't have faith in her plan. There were just too many moving parts. But he would give her credit for thinking outside the box. He was lucky to have her on staff at Lockwood.

Not about to discuss the pros and cons of her plan in front of her, Finn said, "Thank you for your input. We greatly appreciate your efforts. We'll need a little bit to discuss it. In the meantime, you could—"

"But don't you want to hear the rest of my plan?" Holly sent a pleading stare his way.

How could he say no when she turned those big brown eyes his way? He felt his resolve melting.

"Let her finish," Wallace chimed in.

The other men agreed.

Finn nodded at her to proceed.

"Getting the presents from the distribution center to the airstrip will take more transportation."

He was almost afraid to ask. "And what did you have in mind?"

"We'll go public and ask for volunteers."

"More volunteers?" He shook his head. "I don't think so."

"Listen, I know you were hoping to operate under the radar. And I know none of you are in this for the publicity, but if you would reconsider, this project might be bigger and better than before."

He wanted to put a stop to this, but he knew what it was like to be a child with no Christmas presents. Although his lack of presents had nothing to do with his parents' financial standing, it still hurt. He didn't want that to happen to other children, not if he could make a difference.

But he refused to put out a public plea asking for help. He didn't do it for the Mistletoe Ball, which meant so much to him—a continuation of his mother's work and a way to support the foundation seeking a cure to the horrible disease that stole his brother's life. Besides, he was the very last person in the country whom people would want to help. After all of the companies that he'd bought up and spun off into separate entities, causing job consolidation and ultimately downsizing, he was certain people would go out of their way to make sure he failed. He couldn't let that happen with Project Santa.

Finn met her gaze. "I'm not going to make this a publicity campaign."

"But at least hear me out."

He didn't want to. His gut told him she was about to give them a unique but tempting solution to their problem—but it would come at a steep price.

"Go ahead." Wallace spoke up. "Tell us how you would recruit these people?"

"We could start a media page on MyFace." She paused and looked around the table. "Do you know about the social networking service?"

They all nodded.

"Good. Well, it's hugely popular. With a page set up on it specifically for Project Santa, we can post updates and anything else. It even allows for spreadsheets and files. So there can be an official sign-up sheet. Or if you are worried about privacy, I could set up an online form that dumps into a private spreadsheet. In fact, last night when I couldn't sleep I started work on the graphics for the media page."

Caruso smiled at her. "You're a real go-getter. I can see why Finn scooped you up. You must make his life so easy at the office."

"Actually, he and I, well, we don't normally work together."

"Really?" Caruso turned to Finn. "What's wrong with you? How could you let this bright young lady get away from you?"

Finn kept a stony expression, not wanting any of them to get a hint that there was far more to this relationship than either of them was letting on. "I already had a fully capable assistant by the time Holly was hired. She normally works in the legal department, but with my assistant eloping, Holly agreed to fill in."

"And she's done an excellent job with her research." Caruso turned a smile to Holly.

"Yes, she has," Mr. McMurray agreed. "It isn't exactly the most straightforward option, but it definitely deserves further investigation."

Finn was proud that she'd taken the initiative, but he was not expecting the next words out of his mouth. "And we need to give her presentation some serious consideration."

"Agreed." The word echoed around the table.

Holly's hesitant smile broadened into a full-fledged smile that lit up her eyes. "Thank you all for listening to me." Her cloaked gaze met Finn's. "I have work to do. I'll be in my cabin should you need me."

CHAPTER SEVEN

WHAT HAD SHE been thinking?

Holly paced in her cabin, going over the meeting in her mind—more specifically the deepening frown on Finn's face as she'd presented her idea to distribute the gifts. Why had she even bothered? It wasn't like it was part of her job duties—far from it. But there was something about Project Santa that drew her in. She'd wanted to help.

And now she'd made a mess of things. Having Finn upset with her would not help her get the personal recommendation she needed to land the new job and get her the big pay increase she needed to secure her mother's early retirement.

She should have kept the ideas to herself. When would she ever learn? When it came to Finn, she found herself acting first and thinking later. Just like that kiss in his cabin. If they hadn't been interrupted, she knew there would have been no stopping them. Her logic and sanity had gotten lost in the steamy heat of the moment.

Going forward, she would be the perfect employee and that included keeping her hands to herself. She glanced down, realizing she'd been wringing her hands together. She groaned.

She knew Finn was going to shoot down her proposal. His disapproval had been written all over his face. She didn't understand his reaction. It wasn't like he had a better suggestion. No matter what Finn said, she still believed in her grass-roots approach.

Knock-knock.

For a moment she considered ignoring it. She wasn't in any state of mind to deal with Finn. She didn't think it was possible to paste on a smile right now and act like the perfect, obedient assistant. And that would be detrimental to her ultimate goal—leaving Lockwood—leaving Finn.

Knock-knock.

"Holly, I know you're in there. We need to talk." Finn's tone was cool and restrained.

She hesitated. He was obviously not happy with her. And on this yacht, even though it was quite spacious, she wouldn't be able to avoid him for long. So she might as well get it over with.

She took a calming breath, choking down her frustration. On wooden legs, she moved toward the door. Her stomach felt as though a rock had settled in the bottom of it. *You can do this.*

She swung the door open. "Can I do something for you?"

"Yes. I need an explanation of what happened at the meeting." He strode past her and stopped in the middle of the room.

Was it that he didn't like her idea? Or was he upset that it had been her idea and not his? She'd heard rumors that he was a bit of a control freak.

She swallowed hard. "I presented an idea I thought would save Project Santa. What else is there to explain?"

"When did you have time to come up with this idea?"

"Last night when you were playing cards."

His gaze narrowed in on her. "You should have brought it to my attention before making the presentation." His voice rumbled as he spoke. "We should have gone over it together. I'm not accustomed to having employees take the lead on one of my projects without consulting me."

Seriously? This was the thanks she got for going above and beyond her job duties—not to mention sacrificing her sleep—all in order to help him. Maybe it was her lack of sleep or her growing hunger, but she wasn't going to stand by quietly while he railed against her efforts to help.

She straightened her shoulders and lifted her chin. "I'll

have you know that I tried to tell you about my idea this morning, but you didn't have time to listen. And something tells me that isn't what has you riled up. So what is it?"

His heated gaze met hers. "I knew this was going to be a mistake—"

"What? My plan?"

"No. Your idea has some merit. I meant us trying to work together."

"Well, don't blame me. It wasn't my idea."

He sighed. "True enough."

"Wait. Did you say my plan has merit?"

"I did, but I don't think it's feasible."

Her body stiffened as her back teeth ground together. Really? That was what he was going with? Feasible?

She pressed her lips together, holding back her frustration. After all, he was the boss—even if he was being a jerk at the moment.

"I know you're not happy about this decision, but it's a lot to ask of so many pilots, and what happens if they back out at the last minute? It would be a disaster." He glanced down at his deck shoes. "I hope you'll understand. This is just the way it has to be."

"I don't understand." The cork came off her patience and out spewed her frustration and outrage. "I have given you a cost-effective, not to mention a timely solution, to your problem and yet you find every reason it won't work. If you didn't want to go through with Project Santa, why did you start it in the first place?"

"That's not what I said." He pressed his lips into a firm line as his hand came to rest on his trim waist. When she refused to glance away—to back down, he straightened his shoulders as though ready to do battle in the boardroom. "Okay. Your idea could work, but how do you plan on getting the message out to the people about Project Santa and the MyFace page?"

"We'll need a spokesperson."

"Where will you get that?"

She stared pointedly at him. "I'm looking at him."

"Me?"

"Yes, you."

"No way."

"Why not? All you have to do is a few promo spots to se-cure the public's assistance. What's the problem?"

His heated gaze met hers. "Why are you pushing this?"

She implored him with her eyes to truly hear her. "Do you realize the number of children you could help with your gen-erous gifts?" When he refused to engage, she continued. "It would give them hope for the future. It might influence the path they follow in life." And then for good measure she added, "And without your cooperation, they'll never have that chance."

"That's not fair. You can't heap all of that guilt on me."

"Who else should I blame?"

A muscle flexed in his jaw. "You know, I didn't come here to fight with you."

"Then why are you here?"

A tense moment passed before he spoke again. "I wanted to tell you how impressed everyone was with your presen-tation."

"Everyone but you." The words slipped past her lips be-fore she could stop them.

"Holly, that's not true." He raked his fingers through his hair, scattering it. "You don't know how hard this is for me."

"Then why don't you tell me?"

Conflict reflected in his eyes as though he was warring with himself. "I don't want to talk about it."

"Maybe you should. Sometimes getting it all out there helps." She walked over to the couch and had a seat. She patted the cushion next to her. "It might not seem like it at this particular time, but I am a good listener."

His gaze moved from her to the couch. She didn't think

he would do it—trust her with his deeply held secret. But if it stood in the way of his helping with the publicity for Project Santa, then they needed to sort it out.

When he returned his eyes to hers, it was as though she was looking at a haunted person. She hadn't even heard his story yet and still her heart swelled with sympathy for him. Whatever it was, it was big.

"Christmas wasn't always good at our house." His voice held a broken tone to it. "I mean it was when I was little, but not later." He expelled a deep breath.

"I'm sorry for pushing you. I shouldn't have done it—"

"Don't apologize. I understand why you want Project Santa to succeed. And I want the same thing."

"Then trust me. A little publicity is all we need to gain the public's assistance."

"But it has to be without me. Trust me. I'm not the right person to be the face of a charitable event."

"I disagree."

"That's because you don't know me." Pain reflected in his eyes. "Appearances can be deceiving. I'm not the man everyone thinks I am. I'm a fraud."

"A fraud?" She instinctively moved away. "If you aren't Finn Lockwood, who are you?"

"Relax. I'm Finn Lockwood. I'm just not supposed to be the CEO of Lockwood International. I got the job by default."

She was confused. "Who is supposed to be the CEO?"

"My brother."

"Oh." She still didn't understand. "He didn't want the job?"

"He wanted it but he died."

"I'm sorry." She slipped her hand in his. "Sometimes when I have an idea, I don't back off when I should."

For a while, they just sat there in silence. Hand in hand, Holly once again rested her head on Finn's shoulder as though it was natural for them to be snuggled together. Her heart ached for all he'd endured. She felt awful that she'd pushed him to the point where he felt he had to pull the scabs off those old scars.

"You didn't do anything wrong." Finn pulled away and got to his feet. "I should be going. I just wanted you to understand why I can't be the spokesman for Project Santa."

She rolled his words around in her mind, creating a whole new set of questions. She worried her bottom lip. After everything that had been said, she realized that it was best to keep her questions to herself. Enough had been said for one evening.

Finn placed a finger beneath her chin and lifted until they were eye to eye. "What is it?"

She glanced away. "It's nothing."

"Oh, no, you don't get off that easy. What are you thinking?"

She shook her head, refusing to say anything to upset him further. She was certain if she thought about it a bit longer, she'd be able to connect the dots. It was just that right now it was all a bit fuzzy. "It's not important."

"I'm not leaving here until you talk to me. Whatever it is, I promise not to get upset with you. Because that's what you're worried about, isn't it?"

She took a deep breath, trying to figure out how to word this without aggravating him further. "I'm sure it's my fault for not understanding. If I just think it over some more, it'll probably make perfect sense."

He moved his hand from her face and took her hands in his. "Holly, you're rambling. Just spit it out."

She glanced down at their clasped hands. "It's just that I don't understand why the way you became CEO would keep you from getting personally involved with the publicity for Project Santa."

He frowned. See, she knew she should have kept her questions to herself. Clearly she hadn't been listening to him as closely as she'd thought. She prepared herself to feel silly for missing something obvious.

"I don't deserve to take credit for the project. I don't deserve people thinking I'm some sort of great guy."

Really? That was what he thought? "Of course you do. This project was your brainchild. You're the one who brought all of those businessmen together to orchestrate such a generous act. There aren't many people in this world who could have done something like this."

"I'm not a good guy. I've done things—things I'm not proud of."

"We all have. You're being too hard on yourself."

He shook his head. "I wish that was the case. Besides, I'm not even supposed to be doing any of this. This company was supposed to be handed down to Derek, not me. I'm the spare heir. Anything I do is because of my brother's death. I don't deserve any pats on the back or praise."

What in the world had happened to him? Was this some sort of survivor's guilt? That had to be it. She had no idea what it must be like to step into not one but two pairs of shoes—his father's and his brother's.

"I disagree with you."

Finn's brows drew together. "You don't get it. If it weren't for my brother dying, I wouldn't be here."

"Where would you be?"

He shrugged. "I'm not sure. After my brother died, I gave up those dreams and embraced my inevitable role as the leader of Lockwood."

"Did you want to be a policeman or a soldier?" When he shook his head, she asked, "What did you dream of doing with your life?"

"I thought about going into medicine."

"You wanted to be a doctor?"

"I wanted something behind the scenes. I was thinking about medical research. My mother was always going on about how much money her charity work raised to find cures for diseases, but it was never enough. I excelled in math and science—I thought I could make a difference."

"But don't you see? You are making a difference. You gave up your dreams in order to take over the family business, but you've made a point of funding and planning charitable causes. You are a hero, no matter what you tell yourself."

His mouth opened and then he wordlessly closed it. She could tell he was stuck for words. Was it so hard for him to imagine himself as a good guy?

She squeezed his hand. "This is your chance to live up to your dreams."

"How do you get that?"

"You can make a difference to all of those children. You can give them the Christmas you missed out on. Maybe you'll give them a chance to dream of their future. Or at the very least, give them a reason to smile."

His eyes gleamed as though he liked the idea, but then he shook his head. "I'm not hero material." And then his eyes lit up. "But you are. You could be the face of Project Santa."

"Me?" She shook her head. "No one knows me. I won't garner the attention that Finn Lockwood will." Feeling as though she was finally getting through to him, she said, "Please, Finn, trust me. This will all work out. I know you aren't comfortable with the arrangement, but do it for the kids. Be their hero."

There was hesitation written all over his face. "There's no other way?"

"None that I can think of."

The silence stretched on as though Finn was truly rolling around the idea. The longer it took, the more optimistic she became.

His gaze met hers. "Okay. Let's do this."

"Really?" She couldn't quite believe her ears. "You mean it?"

He nodded his head. "As long as the promo is minimized."

"It will be. Trust me."

He didn't look so confident, but in time he'd see that her plan would work. And then a bunch of children wouldn't feel forgotten on Christmas morning. Knowing she'd had a small part in giving them some holiday cheer would make this the best Christmas ever.

"What are you smiling about?"

She was smiling? Yes, she supposed she was. Right now she felt on top of the world. Now that she'd proven her worth to Finn, she thought of asking him for that recommendation letter, but then she decided not to ruin the moment.

"I'm just happy to be part of this meaningful project."

"So where do we begin?" Finn sent her an expectant look.

In that moment all of her excitement and anticipation knotted up with nerves. She'd talked a good game but now it was time to put it all into action. Her stomach churned. She willed it to settle—not that it had any intention of listening to her.

When she didn't say a word, Finn spoke up. "Where do we start?"

The *we* in his question struck her. They were now a team. Not allowing herself to dwell on this new bond, she asked, "What about your guests? Shouldn't you be with them?"

"McMurray said he wasn't feeling so good and went to lie down. The other guys are taking in some sun and playing cards. So I'm all yours."

She eyed him up, surprised by his roll-up-his-sleeves-and-dive-in attitude. "The first place we start is on MyFace and work on recruiting additional pilots. Do you have a MyFace account?"

"No. I'll get my laptop." He got to his feet and headed for the door. He paused in the doorway and turned back to her. "On second thought, why don't you bring your laptop and work in my suite? It's a lot bigger."

Holly paused. The last time she'd been in his room, work had been the very last thing on either of their minds. The memory of him pulling her close, of his lips moving hungrily over hers, sent her heart pounding. She vividly remembered how he'd awakened her long-neglected body. Their arms had been entangled. Their breath had intermingled. And any rational thoughts had fled the room.

"I know what you're thinking."

Heat flared in her cheeks. *Are my thoughts that transparent?*

"But don't worry, it won't happen again. You have my word."

Maybe I can trust you, but it's me that I'm worried about.

CHAPTER EIGHT

SHE AMAZED HIM.

Finn awoke the next morning thinking of Holly. They'd worked together until late the night before. She had truly impressed him—which wasn't an easy feat. To top it off, she was efficient and organized. He knew she was good at her job, but he had no idea just how talented she was until last night.

They'd taken a long break for dinner with his associates. They updated them on all they'd accomplished and what Holly hoped to achieve over the next few days. The men promised to do their part to ensure the success of Project Santa, including putting out a call for volunteers to their employees and their families.

And to Finn's shock the two men who weren't active on social media were open to having Holly assist them with setting up a personal MyFace account. Everyone wanted to do their part to promote the project so that it was a success.

Finn slipped out of bed and quietly padded to the shower. With Project Santa underway, he had to concentrate on to-day's business agenda. He had a business venture that he wanted to entice these men to invest in. And thanks to Holly, everyone appeared to be in fine spirits. He hoped to capitalize on it.

Today he'd switched from his dress shorts and polos to slacks and a dress shirt. He couldn't help it. When he wanted to take charge of a business meeting, he wanted to look the part, too. He supposed that was something his father had taught him. Though his father had spiraled out of control after his brother's death, before that he was a pretty good guy, just a bit driven. He supposed his father was no more a workaholic than himself.

Finn straightened the collar of his light blue shirt with vertical white stripes sans the tie. Then he turned up the cuffs. After placing his Rolex on his wrist, he was ready to get down to business. Now he just needed Holly to take some notes.

He headed down the passageway to her cabin and knocked. There was no answer.

"Holly, are you in there?"

Knock-knock.

"Holly?"

That was strange. When they'd parted for the evening, they'd agreed to get together first thing in the morning to go over today's agenda. And then he recalled her picking her way through her dinner. Maybe he should be sure she was okay.

He tried the doorknob. It wasn't locked. He opened it a crack. "Holly, I'm coming in."

No response.

He hesitantly opened the door, not sure what he expected to find. He breathed easier when he found her bed empty. Before he could react, the bathroom door swung open and she came rushing out.

Dressed in a short pink nightie, she was a bit hunched over. Her arm was clutched over her stomach.

"Holly?"

She jumped. Her head swung around to face him. The color leached from her face. He wasn't sure if the lack of coloring was the result of his startling her or if it was because she didn't feel well.

"What are you doing here?"

"Sorry. I didn't mean to startle you. I…uh, well, we were supposed to meet up this morning. And when you didn't answer the door, I got worried. I came in to make sure you're all right."

Holly glanced down at herself as though realizing her lack of clothing. She moved to the bed and slid under the sheets. "I'm fine."

"You don't look fine."

"Well, thanks. You sure know how to make a girl feel better." She frowned at him.

"That's not what I meant. I…uh, just meant you don't look like yourself. What can I get for you?"

"Nothing."

"Are you sure? Maybe some eggs?" Was it possible that her pale face just turned a ghastly shade of green? She vehemently shook her head. Okay. Definitely no eggs. "How about toast?"

Again she shook her head. "No food. Not now."

"Are you sick?"

"No." Her answer came too quickly.

"Something is wrong or you wouldn't be curled up in bed."

"It's just the sway of the yacht. I'm not used to it."

He planted his hands on his waist. He supposed that was a reasonable explanation. "You aren't the only one with a bout of motion sickness. McMurray still isn't well. I guess my sailing expedition wasn't such a good idea."

"It was a great idea. And I'll be up on deck shortly."

"Take the morning off and rest—"

"No. I'm already feeling better. Just give me a bit to get ready."

"Why must you always be so stubborn?"

She sent him a scowl. "I'm not stubborn. It isn't like you know me that well."

"Since we started working together, I've learned a lot about you."

"Like what?"

He sighed but then decided to be truthful with her. "I know that you're honest. You're a hard worker. And you go above and beyond what is asked of you in order to do a good job."

A smile bloomed on her still-pale face. "Anything else?"

"I know you can be passionate—about causes you believe in. And sometimes you push too hard if you think it will help someone else."

She eyed him up. "You really believe all of that nice stuff about me? You're not saying it because you feel sorry for me, are you?"

Was she hunting for more compliments? He searched her eyes and found a gleam of uncertainty. He had to wonder, if only to himself, how someone so talented and sure of herself when it came to business could be so insecure behind closed doors.

"Yes, I meant everything I said. You're very talented."

Holly worried her bottom lip. When his gaze met hers, she glanced away. What did she have on her mind? Something told him whatever it was he wasn't going to like it. But they might as well get it over with.

"What else do you have on your mind?"

She blinked as though considering her options. Then she sat up straight, letting the sheet pool around her waist. He inwardly groaned as her nightie was not exactly conservative, and that was not something he needed to be contemplating at this moment.

Stay focused on the conversation! Don't let your eyes dip. Focus on her face.

Holly lifted her chin. "I would like to know if you'd write me a personal recommendation."

"Recommendation? For what?"

She visibly swallowed. The muscles in her slender neck worked in unison. "I have an inside source who says a prime opportunity is about to open up and I'd like to apply for the position."

"No problem. Just tell me what department it is and I'll make it happen. But I thought you liked working in the legal department."

"I did—I mean I do. But you don't understand. This job isn't within Lockwood."

He had to admit that he hadn't seen that one coming. And for a man that prided himself on being able to plan ahead, this was a bit much to swallow. "But I don't understand. You like your job, so this has to be about us."

Her slender shoulders rose and fell. "It's too complicated for me to stay on at Lockwood."

"You mean the kiss the other evening, don't you?"

Her gaze didn't quite meet his. "It would just be easier if I were to work elsewhere."

"When would you be taking this new position?"

"At the beginning of the year. So you don't have to worry about Project Santa. It will be completed before I leave and I'll be out of Lockwood before you return to New York."

"Sounds awfully convenient." His voice took on a disgruntled tone.

He didn't like the thought of Holly going to such lengths to keep her path from crossing his. Up until this trip, they'd done so well avoiding each other at the office. He had to admit a few times he'd hoped to bump into her in a hallway or the elevator, but that had never happened.

Holly was smart for wanting to get away from him. When his ex-fiancée hadn't been able to deal with his moods and distance, she'd left. He'd never blamed her. It was what he'd deserved. He should be relieved that Holly wanted to move on, but he couldn't work up the emotion.

He told himself that he didn't want to see her go because she was a good worker. She was smart and a go-getter. She wasn't afraid to think outside the box. His company needed more innovative people like her.

Holly smoothed the cream-colored sheet as though sorting her thoughts. "Listen, I know this comes as a surprise, but I really do think it would be for the best. It isn't like either one of us wants a serious relationship. You have your company to focus on."

"And what do you have?" He knew there was more to this request than she was saying, perhaps something even beyond what was going on between the two of them. Because if her reasons extended beyond the attraction between them, then he could fix it and she would stay, he hoped.

"I have my work, and this new position will help me to grow and to take on greater responsibility."

"And you can't do that at Lockwood?"

She shrugged, letting him know that she'd already dismissed that option.

Without Holly to liven things up, he would return to a downright boring existence. Before he handed over the golden ticket to another position, he needed more time to think this over. Surely there had to be a way to persuade her into staying.

"You've caught me off guard. Can I have some time to think over your request?"

"Of course. But don't take too long. Once word gets out about the opening, the candidates will flood the office with résumés."

He could see she'd given this a lot of thought and her mind was made up. "Just tell me one thing and be honest. Is this because you're trying to get away from me?"

Her gaze met his. "Maybe. Partly. But it's an amazing opportunity and I don't want to miss out on it."

"Would you be willing to tell me what the position is?"

"That would be telling you two things and you said you'd only ask one thing."

"And so I did." He sighed. "This isn't over."

"I didn't think that it was."

"I'll go get you some ginger ale and crackers."

"You don't have to do that. You have a business meeting to attend."

"Not before I see that you're cared for."

And with that he made a hasty exit from the cabin, still digesting the news. It left an uneasy feeling in his gut. And this was why he never got involved with employees of Lockwood. It made things sticky and awkward, not to mention he couldn't afford to lose such talent.

CHAPTER NINE

IT WAS SO good to be back on solid ground.

The next morning Holly stood on the balcony of Finn's beach house that was more like a mansion. He'd just escorted his last guest to the helipad. Their sailing trip had been cut short due to the rough waters. She thought for sure Finn would be upset, but he took it all in stride.

She shouldn't be standing here. There was work to be done on Project Santa—work that could be done from anywhere in the world, including New York.

The sound of footsteps caused her to turn around. Finn stopped at the edge of the deck. He didn't smile and the look in his eyes was unreadable.

"Did everyone get off okay?"

"They did."

The silence between them dragged on. Finn obviously had something on his mind. Maybe this was her chance to broach the subject of her leaving.

She turned to him.

"I was thinking I should get to work. You know, there's no reason I can't complete Project Santa in New York. I can make my travel arrangements and be out of your way shortly."

"You're not in my way." His voice dropped to a serious tone. "Have I somehow made you feel unwelcome?"

"Well, no, but I just thought that, ah, well, there's no point in me staying on the island. That is, unless you still need my assistance."

"You're right." His voice was calm and even. "Any work from here on out can be done via phone or the internet."

His sudden agreement stung. She knew she should be relieved, but she was conflicted. His eagerness to see her gone almost felt as though she was being dismissed—as though she hadn't quite measured up as his PA. Was that what he was thinking? Or had he merely grown tired of her like the other men in her life had done?

"I'll pack my bags and leave tomorrow."

She moved swiftly from the large deck and into the cool interior of the house. The sooner she got off this island, the better. She'd forget about Finn and how every time she was around him she wanted to follow up their kiss with another and another.

A new job was just what she needed. It'd give her the time and space to get over this silly crush she had on Finn. Because that was all it was, a crush. Nothing more.

So much for Holly's departure and having his life return to normal.

She was sick again.

Finn paced back and forth in his study.

He didn't care what Holly said, it obviously wasn't sea-sickness any longer. Her illness could be anything, including something serious. He hadn't gotten a bit of work done all morning. At least nothing worthwhile. And now that lunch was over and Holly hadn't shown up, he wasn't sure what to do. He'd never been in a position of worrying about someone else.

When his brother had been sick, it had been his parents who'd done most of the worrying and the caretaking. And then there had been his great-aunt who'd taken him in after his parents' deaths, but she was made of hearty stock or so she'd liked to tell him. She'd barely been sick a day while he'd known her. Even on the few times she'd gotten the sniffles, she carried on, doing what needed to be done until her final breath.

But he couldn't ignore how poorly Holly looked. And

her appetite at best was iffy. Then a thought came to him. He'd take a tray of food to her room. There had to be something she could eat.

When he entered the kitchen, Maria, his cook/housekeeper, glanced up from where she was pulling spices to prepare the evening dinner. "Can I get you something?"

Finn shook his head. "Don't let me bother you. I'm just going to put together a tray to take to Miss Abrams."

"I can do it for you."

"I've got it." There was a firm tone to his voice, more so than he'd intended. He just needed to do this on his own. "Sorry. I'm just a little worried."

Maria nodded as in understanding before turning back to her work.

Finn raided the fridge, settling on sandwich makings. It was what he ate late at night. And then he thought of something that Holly might enjoy. It was something his aunt swore by. Tea. "Maria, do we have some tea around here?"

The older woman smiled and nodded as though at last happy to be able to do something to help.

Between the two of them, they put together an extensive tray of food plus spearmint tea. And just to be on the safe side, he added a glass of ginger ale and crackers. As an afterthought, he snagged one of the pink rosebuds from the bouquet on the dining room table, slipped it into a bud vase and added it to the full tray. Hopefully this would cheer Holly up.

He strode down the hallway, up the steps and down another hallway until he stopped in front of her door. He tapped his knuckles on the door.

"Holly, it's me."

Within seconds, she pulled open the door. Her hair was mussed up and there was a sleepy look on her face. Her gaze lowered to the tray. "What's all of this?"

"It's for you. I noticed you missed lunch. I thought this might tide you over until dinner."

"Till dinner? I think that amount of food could last me for the next couple of days."

He glanced down at the sandwich. "I wasn't sure what meat and cheese you prefer so I added a little of everything. I figured you could just take off what you don't like."

"And the chips, fruit, vegetables and dip. Is there anything you forgot?"

He glanced over the tray and then a thought came to him. "I forgot to add some soup. Would you like some?"

"I think I'll get by with what you brought me."

A smile lifted her lips, easing the tired, stressed lines on her face. His gaze moved past her and trailed around the room, surprised to find that her laptop was closed. And then he spied the bed with the wrinkled comforter and the indent on the pillow. She'd been lying down.

"I'll put it over here." He moved toward the desk in the corner of her room. When she didn't follow him, he turned back to her. There were shadows under her eyes and her face was void of color. "Holly—"

She ran out of the room. She sent the bathroom door slamming shut.

That was it. He was done waiting for this bug or whatever was ailing her to pass. He pulled his cell phone from his pocket and requested that the chopper transport them to the big island where there would be medical help.

He didn't care how much she protested, this simply couldn't go on. There was something seriously wrong here. And he was worried—really worried.

"Finn, don't forget your promise."

"I won't." He stared straight ahead as he searched for a parking spot on the big island.

Before they flew here, Holly had extracted a promise from him. If she agreed to this totally unnecessary doctor's appointment, he would help her catch the next flight home.

She was certain whatever was plaguing her was no more than a flu bug. No big deal. She had no idea why Finn was so concerned.

Being an hour early for her appointment, Holly took advantage of the opportunity to meander through the colorful shops and the intriguing stands along the street. And in the end, it was a productive visit as she bought a few gifts.

When it was time to head to the clinic, Holly pleaded that it wasn't necessary. She was feeling better, but Finn insisted, reminding her that they had an agreement. And so they did. It also meant that she was almost homeward bound…just as soon as this appointment was concluded. She'd even packed her bag and brought it with her.

In the doctor's office Holly completed the paperwork and then they took her vital statistics. An older doctor examined her. He did a lot of hemming and hawing, but he gave her no insight into what those sounds meant. When she pointedly asked him what was wrong with her, he told her that he'd need to order a couple of tests.

Tests? That doesn't sound good.

She was feeling better. That had to be a good sign. But why was the doctor being so closemouthed? Although she recalled when her mother had suffered a stroke, trying to get information out of doctors was nearly impossible until they were ready to speak to you.

So she waited, but not alone. With her exam over, she invited Finn back to the room so he could hear with his own ears that she was fine. She was certain the doctor was only being cautious.

In the bright light, she noticed that Finn didn't look quite like himself. "Are you feeling all right?"

His gaze met hers. "I'm fine. It's you we should worry about."

She studied him a bit more. His face was pale and his eyes were dull. There was definitely something wrong with him.

"Oh, no, have I made you sick, too?"

He waved away her worry. "I'm like my great-aunt. I don't get sick."

"I don't believe you."

Finn's jaw tensed and a muscle in his cheek twitched, but he didn't argue with her. Okay, so maybe she was pushing it a bit. Doctor's offices made her uptight.

"I'm sorry," she said. "I didn't mean anything by that. I guess I don't do well with doctors."

The lines on Finn's handsome face smoothed out. "Why? What happened?"

She shrugged. "You don't want to hear about it."

"Sure, I do. That is, if you'll tell me."

Oh, well, what else did they have to do while waiting for the test results? There weren't even any glossy magazines in the small room. So while she sat on the exam table, Finn took a seat on the only chair in the room.

"It was a couple of days after you and I, you know, after—"

"The night we spent together?"

She nodded. "Yes, that. Well, I got a call from my mother's work. They were taking my mother to the hospital." She paused, recalling that frantic phone call when life as she knew it had come to a sudden standstill. "I'd never been so scared. I didn't know what was going on. I just knew an ambulance had been called for my mother. That's never a good sign."

"I'm sorry. I didn't know. I… I would have done something."

She glanced at him. "There was nothing for you to do. Remember, we agreed to stay clear of each other."

"Even so, I would have been there for you, if you'd have called me."

Holly shook her head. "I was fine. But thanks."

"I'm sure you had the rest of your family and friends to keep you company."

Holly shrugged. "I was fine."

He arched a brow. "When you said that the first time, I didn't believe you. And I don't believe it this time, either."

"Okay. I wasn't fine. I was scared to death. Is that what you want to hear?"

"No, it isn't what I want to hear. But I'm glad you're finally being honest with me."

Her gaze met his. "Why? It isn't like there's anything between us. At least, not anymore."

"Is that the truth? Or are you trying to convince yourself that you don't feel anything for me?"

She inwardly groaned. Why did everything have to be so complicated where Finn was concerned? Why couldn't things be simple, like her life had been before she'd walked into his office all those weeks ago?

CHAPTER TEN

NOW, WHY HAD he gone and asked her if she had feelings for him?

Finn leaned his head back and sighed. It wasn't like he wanted to pick up where they'd left off. It didn't matter that they had chemistry and lots of it. In time, he'd forget about her sweet kisses and gentle caresses. He had to—she was better off without him.

He'd tried having a real relationship once. Talk about a mess. He wasn't going to repeat that mistake. Not that Holly was anything like Meryl. Not at all.

"Holly—"

The exam room door swung open. The doctor strode in and closed the door behind him. He lowered his reading glasses to the bridge of his nose. His dark head bent over a piece of paper. When he glanced up, his gaze immediately landed on Finn.

"Oh, hello." The doctor's puzzled gaze moved to Holly.

"It's okay. You can talk in front of him."

The doctor hesitated.

Holly sent the doctor a reassuring smile. "Finn's the one who insisted on bringing me here, and I just want to show him that he was overreacting."

"If you're sure."

She smiled and nodded.

"Okay then. I have the results back. It's what I initially suspected. You have morning sickness."

"Morning sickness? You mean I'm pregnant?" Holly vocalized Finn's stunned thoughts.

The doctor's bushy brows drew together. "I thought you knew."

Holly turned to Finn, the color in her face leaching away,

but no words crossed her lips. That was okay because for once, Finn couldn't think of anything to say, at least nothing that would make much sense.

A baby. We're having a baby.

Disbelief. Surprise. Excitement. Anger. It all balled together and washed over Finn.

Holly stared at him as though expecting him to say something, anything. But he didn't dare. Not yet. Not until he had his emotions under control. One wrong word and he wouldn't be able to rebound from it. And to be honest, he was stuck on six little—life-changing—words.

I'm going to be a father. I'm going to be a father.

Holly turned her attention back to the doctor. "You're sure? About the baby, that is."

The doctor's gaze moved to Finn and then back to her. The question was in his eyes, but he didn't vocalize it.

"Yes, he's the father."

Finn realized this was another of those moments where he should speak, but his mind drew a blank. It was though there was this pink-and-blue neon sign flashing in his mind that said *baby.*

"I'm one hundred percent certain you're pregnant." The doctor's forehead scrunched up. "I take it you have your doubts."

"Well, I, um—" she glanced at Finn before turning back to the doctor "—had my period since we were together. Granted it was light."

"Recently?"

"The week before last."

"Was there any cramping associated with it?"

She shook her head. "None that I recall."

"A little spotting is not uncommon. Have you had any spotting since then?"

"No. I'm just really tired. Are…are you sure everything is okay with the baby?"

"I'll be honest, you're still in your first trimester, which means the risk of miscarriage is higher. But I didn't tell you that to worry you. I just want you to realize that taking care of yourself is of the utmost importance."

"The baby." Her heart was racing so fast. "It's okay, right?"

"At this point, yes. I've arranged for a sonogram." He moved to the counter to retrieve a stack of literature. "You might like to read over these. They're about prenatal care and what to expect over the next several months. I'll be back."

Finn paced. Neither spoke as they each tried to grasp the news. Seconds turned to minutes. At last, Finn sank into the chair, feeling emotionally wiped out. His gaze moved to Holly but she appeared engrossed in a baby magazine the doctor had given her.

Where was the doctor? Had he forgotten them?

As though Finn's thoughts had summoned the man, the door swung open. A nurse walked in. Her eyes widened at the sight of Finn.

The nurse handed Holly a pink gown. "The straps go in the front." Then the nurse turned to him. "You might want to wait outside."

"I think you're right." That was it. Finn was out of there. He had no idea what was involved with a sonogram, but he'd give Holly her privacy.

When he reached the waiting room, he was tempted to keep going. In here he felt as though he couldn't quite catch his breath. Outside, in the fresh air, he would be able to breathe again. But he didn't want to move that far from Holly. What if she needed him?

And so he remained in the waiting room. He picked up a baby magazine, glanced at the cover and put it back down. He picked up another magazine, but it was for women. He put it down, too.

The door he'd just exited opened. A different nurse poked her head out. "Mr. Lockwood."

He approached her, not having a clue what she wanted. "I'm Mr. Lockwood."

"If you would come with me, sir." She led him back to Holly's exam room.

When he stood in the doorway, he found Holly lying on the exam table with a large sheet draped over her legs. He did not want to be here. He shouldn't be here.

Holly held her hand out to him. "Come see our baby."

He did want to see the baby. It would make it real for him. He moved to Holly's side, all the while keeping his gaze straight ahead, focused on the monitor. He slipped his hand in hers, finding her fingers cold. He assumed it was nerves. He sandwiched her hand between both of his, hoping to warm her up a little.

In no time at all, there was a fuzzy image on the monitor. Finn watched intently, trying to make out his child. And then it was there. It didn't look much like a baby at this point, but the doctor pointed out the head and spine.

"Wait a second, I need to check one more thing."

The doctor made an adjustment. Holly's fingers tightened their hold on Finn. Her worried gaze met his. Was there something wrong with their child?

Finn fervently hoped not. He just didn't think he could go through all his parents had endured with his brother. It was an experience he'd never forget.

"Okay." The doctor's voice rose. "Here we go. Just as I suspected."

Finn couldn't be left in the dark. He had to know what they were facing. "What's the matter?"

The doctor smiled up at him. "Nothing at all. You are having twins."

"Twins!" Holly said it at the same time as Finn.

"Yes, see here." The doctor showed them both babies.

It was the most amazing thing Finn had ever witnessed in his life. Twins. Who'd have thought? His vision started to blur, causing him to blink repeatedly. He was going to be a father—twice over.

He glanced down at Holly. A tear streamed down her cheek. His gut clenched. Was that a sign of joy or unhappiness? It was hard for him to tell. And then she turned and smiled at him. He released the pent-up breath in his lungs.

Holly squeezed his hand. "Did you see that? Those are our babies."

"I saw."

The doctor cleared his throat. "Well, you'll want to see your OB/GYN as soon as possible. But in the meantime, you need some rest and lots of fluids."

"Rest?"

"Yes and fluids. You have to be careful not to become dehydrated with the morning sickness."

"Okay. Whatever you say. I still can't believe I missed all of the signs."

"You aren't the first. Some women are in labor before they realize they are pregnant. These things happen."

Finn followed the doctor into the hallway while Holly got dressed. When they reentered the room, Holly looked different. Was it possible there was a bit of a glow about her? Or was he imagining things?

The doctor went over some suggestions on how to minimize her morning sickness and gave her a bottle of prenatal vitamins to get her started. "If you have any problems while you're in the islands, feel free to come back. I'm always here."

"I was planning to fly to New York today or tomorrow. Would that be all right?"

"I'd like to see you rested and hydrated before you travel. Get your morning sickness under control first."

Finn could feel everyone's attention turning his way, but he continued to study the random pattern of the floor tiles. He had nothing to contribute to this conversation, not at this point. This sudden turn of events was something he'd never envisioned.

The door opened and closed.

"Finn, are you okay?"

He glanced up, finding that he was alone with Holly. "Okay? No."

Her lips formed an O. "Can I say or do anything?"

He shook his head. He should be the one reassuring her, letting her know this was all going to be all right, but he couldn't lie to her. He had no idea how any of this was going to be all right. He was the last person in the world who should be a father. In fact, up until this point, he'd intended to leave all of his estate to designated charities.

But now, wow, everything had just changed. He raked his fingers through his hair. He had to rethink everything.

Pull it together. She's expecting me to say something.

He lifted his head and met her worried gaze that shimmered with unshed tears. That was the last thing he'd expected. Holly was always so strong and sure of what she wanted. Her tears socked him in the gut, jarring him back to reality. She was just as scared as he was, if not more so.

Oh, boy, were his children in big trouble here. Neither Holly nor himself was prepared to be a parent. They had so much to learn and so little time.

Finn stood. "Let's go back to the island."

Her worried gaze met his. "But what about New York?"

"You heard the doctor. You need to rest first." He held his hand out to her.

She hesitated but then grasped his hand.

He didn't know what the future held, but for now they were in it together. For better. Or for worse.

CHAPTER ELEVEN

WHAT WERE THEY supposed to do now?

A few days after returning from their trip to the big island, Holly was starting to feel better. The suggestions the doctor had given her for morning sickness were helping. And she'd been monitoring her fluid intake.

She was still trying to come to terms with the fact that she was pregnant. There was no question in her mind about keeping the babies, but that was the only thing she knew for sure.

Maria and Emilio had been called away from the island. This meant Holly and Finn had the entire island to themselves. In another time, that might have been exciting, even romantic, but right now, they had serious matters on their minds.

She paced back and forth in the study. Where would she live? How would she manage a job, helping out her mother and being a mom all on her own? And where did this leave her and Finn?

The questions continued to whirl around in her mind. She would figure it out—she had to—because she wasn't going to fall back on Finn. She'd counted on two men in her life and they'd both failed her. She knew better this time around. She could only count on herself.

Deciding she wasn't going to get any more work done, she headed for the kitchen. She needed something to do with her hands and she had an urge for something sweet.

As she searched the cabinets, looking for something to appease her craving, her thoughts turned to Finn. He'd barely spoken to her since they left the doctor's office. The occasional nod or grunt was about as much as she got out of him.

She couldn't blame him. It was a lot to adjust to. Her mind was still spinning. Her hand ran over her abdomen.

A baby. No, two babies. Inside her. Wow!

"How are you feeling?" Finn asked.

Four whole words strung together. She would take that as a positive sign. "Better."

"And the babies?"

"Are perfectly fine." She bent over to retrieve a cookie sheet from the cabinet.

"I can get that for you." Finn rushed around the counter with his hands outstretched.

"I can manage." She glared at him until he retreated to the other side of the counter.

She placed the cookie sheet on the counter before turning on the oven. "Did you need something?"

"You're planning to bake? Now?"

"Sure. Why not? I have a craving."

"Isn't it a little early for those?"

She sighed. Why did he have to pick now of all times to get chatty? She just wanted to eat some sugary goodness in peace. "Not that kind of craving."

"Then what kind?"

What was up with him? He'd never been so curious about her dietary habits before. Or maybe he was just attempting to be friendly and she was being supersensitive. She choked down her agitation, planning to give him the benefit of the doubt.

"These are cravings that I get when I'm stressed out." She pulled open the door on the stainless-steel fridge and withdrew a roll of premade cookie dough. "Do you want some cookies?"

"If you're stressed about Project Santa—?"

"It's not that!"

His eyes widened. "Oh. I see."

This was another opening for him to discuss the big pink

or perhaps blue elephant in the room. And yet, he said nothing. Her gaze met his and he glanced away. Was this his way of telling her that he wasn't interested in being a father?

She placed the package of cookie dough on the counter before moving to the oven to adjust the temperature. Next, she needed a cutting board. There had to be one around here somewhere. The kitchen was equipped with absolutely everything. At last, she spotted a small pineapple-shaped board propped against the stone backsplash.

With the cutting board and a knife in hand, she moved back to the counter. "I'll have some reindeer cookies ready in no time. I thought about some hot chocolate with the little marshmallows, but it's a little warm around here for that."

"Thanks. But I'll pass on the cookies. I have some emails I need to get to. By the way, do you have a copy of the Cutter contract?"

"I do. It's in my room. Just let me finish putting these cookies on the tray." She put a dozen on the tray and slipped it in the oven. "Okay. There." She turned back to him. "Stay here and I'll be right back."

She rushed to her spacious guest room that overlooked the ocean. It was a spectacular view. She was tempted to take a dip in the sea or at the very least walk along the beach, letting her feet get wet. Maybe she'd do it later, after she was done working for the day.

Turning away from the window, her gaze strayed over the colorful packages she'd brought back from the big island. She'd splurged a bit, buying a little something for everyone, including her half-sisters, Suzie and Kristi.

Holly worried her bottom lip. She always tried so hard to find something that would impress them and each year, she'd failed. Thankfully she'd bought the gifts before her doctor's appointment because afterward she hadn't been in a holly-jolly spirit. The bikinis, sunglasses, flip-flops and a cover-up with the name of the island were placed in yellow tissue-paper-lined shopping bags. The girls would be all set for summer. About the same time she was giving birth.

With a sigh, Holly continued her hunt for the contract. On top of the dresser, she found the file folder. She pulled it out from beneath a stack of papers and an expandable folder when the back of her hand struck the lamp. Before she could stop it, the lamp toppled over.

Holly gasped as it landed on the floor and shattered, sending shards of glass all over the room. As she knelt down to clean up the mess, she muttered to herself. It was then that she heard rapid footsteps in the hallway.

"What happened?" Finn's voice carried a note of concern. "Are you okay?"

"I am. But the same can't be said for the lamp."

"I'm not worried about it." His concerned gaze met hers.

"I'll have this cleaned up in no time. Your contract is on the edge of the dresser."

When he stepped forward, she thought it was to retrieve the contract. However, the next thing she knew, he knelt down beside her.

"What are you doing?" she asked, not quite believing her eyes.

"Helping you."

"I don't need your help—"

"Well, you better get used to it because I plan to help with these babies."

It wasn't a question. It was an emphatic statement.

Her stomach churned. She was losing her control—her independence. She was about to lose her sense of security because her life would no longer be her own—Finn and the babies would now be a part of it—forever.

Holly sucked in a deep breath, hoping it'd slow the rapid pounding of her heart.

"Did you cut yourself on the broken glass?" Finn glanced down at her hands.

"I'm fine." She got to her feet, needing some distance from him. And then she smelled something. She sniffed again. "Oh, no! The cookies."

She rushed to the kitchen and swung the oven door open. The Christmas cookies were all brown and burnt. With Finn hovering about, she'd forgotten to turn on the timer. She groaned aloud, not caring if he heard her or not.

She turned to the garbage and dumped the cookies in it. Her gaze blurred. The memory of Finn's words and the knowledge that life would never be the same made her feel off-kilter and scared. What were they supposed to do now?

CHAPTER TWELVE

HE HAD TO do something, but what?

The next evening, Finn did his best to concentrate on the details of a potential acquisition for Lockwood. Try as he might, his thoughts kept straying back to Holly and the babies. This was the time when his family would be invaluable. A deep sadness came over him, realizing that his children would never know his parents or his brother, Derek. In that moment he knew that it would be his responsibility to tell his children about their past—about their grandparents and uncle. Finn didn't take the notion lightly.

He glanced across the study to where Holly was sitting on the couch, working on her laptop. She'd been feeling better, which was a relief. Whatever the doctor had told her to do was helping. Now they could focus on the future.

His gaze moved to the windows behind her. The day was gray and glum just like his mood. He knew what needed to be done. They needed to get married.

He'd wrestled with the thought for days now. And it was the only solution that made sense. Although, he wasn't ready to get down on one knee and lay his heart on the line. Just the thought of loving someone else and losing them made his blood run cold. No, it was best their marriage was based on something more reliable—common goals.

The welfare of their children would be the tie that bound them. Finn's chest tightened when he realized that he knew less than nothing about babies. He would need help and lots of it. That was where Holly came in. He needed her guidance if he wanted to be the perfect parent—or as close to it as possible. Without her, he wouldn't even know where to start.

He assured himself that it would all work out. After all,

Holly was the mother to the Lockwood heirs. Their fates had been sealed as soon as she became pregnant. They would have to marry. And he would do his utmost to keep his family safe.

Holly leaned back. "I'm almost finished with the last details for Project Santa. I've reviewed the list of volunteers, state by state and city by city. I've been trying to determine whether there are enough volunteers to transport the gifts from the airports to the designated outreach centers."

Finn welcomed the distraction. "And what have you determined?"

"I think we need a few more drivers. I've already posted a request on MyFace. I'll wait and see what the response is before I take further steps."

"Good. It sounds like you have everything under control."

The fact that they worked well together was another thing they could build on. It would give their marriage a firm foundation. Because he just couldn't open his heart—he couldn't take that risk again.

A gust of wind made a shutter on the house rattle, jarring Finn from his thoughts. It was really picking up out there. So much for the sunshine in paradise. It looked like they'd soon be in for some rain.

"Finn, we need to talk." The banging continued, causing Holly to glance around. "What was that pounding sound?"

"I think it's a shutter that needs tightening."

Holly closed her laptop and set it aside. She got to her feet and moved to the window as though to inspect the problem. "Do you have a screwdriver and a ladder?"

"Yes, but why?"

"I'll go fix it."

"You?"

She frowned at him. "Yes, me. If you haven't noticed, I'm not one to sit around helplessly and wait for some guy to come take care of me."

"But you're pregnant and have doctor's orders to rest. You shouldn't be climbing on ladders. I'll take care of it later."

She sighed loudly. "I've been following his orders and I'm feeling much better. But if you insist, I'll leave the house repairs to you. Besides, there's something else we need to discuss."

"Is there another problem with Project Santa?"

"No. It's not that." She averted her gaze. "Remember how I asked you for a letter of recommendation?"

Why would she bring that up now? Surely she wasn't still considering it. Everything had changed what with the babies and all. "I remember."

Her gaze lifted to meet his. "Have you made a decision?"

"I didn't think it was still an issue."

"Why not?"

"Because you won't be leaving Lockwood, unless of course you want to stay home with the babies, which I'd totally understand. They are certainly going to be a handful and then some."

"Why do you think I won't leave to take that new job?"

Finn sent her a very puzzled look. "Because you're carrying the Lockwood heirs. And soon we'll be married—"

"Married?" Holly took a step back.

What was Finn talking about? They weren't getting married. Not now. Not ever.

"Of course. It's the next logical step—"

"No." She shook her head as her heart raced and her hands grew clammy. "It isn't logical and it certainly isn't my next step. You never even asked me, not that I want you to or anything."

"I thought it was implied."

"Implied? Maybe in your mind, but certainly not in mine. I'm not marrying you. I'm not going to marry anyone."

"Of course you are." His voice rumbled with irritation.

"This isn't the Stone Age. A woman can be pregnant without a husband. There are plenty of loving, single mothers in this world. Take a look around your office building. You'll find quite a few. But you won't find me there after the first of the year."

Had she really just said that? Oh, my. She'd gotten a little ahead of herself. What if he turned his back and walked away without giving her the recommendation? And she didn't have the job. It was still iffy at best. And without her position at Lockwood to fall back on, how would she support herself much less the babies and her mother?

"You're really serious about leaving, aren't you?"

She nodded, afraid to open her mouth again and make the situation worse.

"Do you really dislike me that much?"

"No! Not at all." In fact, it was quite the opposite.

She worried the inside of her lower lip as she glanced toward the window. The wind had picked up, whipping the fronds of the palm trees to and fro. She did not want to answer this question. Not at all.

"Holly?" Finn got to his feet and came to stand in front of her. "Why are you doing this? Why are you trying to drive us apart?"

"You...you're making this sound personal and it isn't." Heat rushed up her neck and made her face feel as though she'd been lying in the sun all day with no sunscreen.

"It is personal. It couldn't be more personal."

"No, it isn't. It's not like you and I, like we're involved."

"I don't know your definition of involved, but I don't think it gets much more involved than you carrying my babies."

"Finn, we both agreed after that night together that we wouldn't have anything to do with each other. We mutually decided that going our separate ways was for the best—for both of us."

"That was before."

"The pregnancy is a complication. I'll admit that. But we can work out an arrangement with the babies. We don't have to live out of each other's back pockets."

"I don't want to live in your back pocket. I want to provide a home for my children and their mother—"

"I don't need you to take care of me or the babies. I can manage on my own."

"But the point is you don't have to. I'm here to help. We can help each other."

She shook her head. "A marriage of convenience won't work."

"Sure it will, if we want it to."

Holly crossed her arms. "Why are you so certain you're right? It's not like we're in love. This thing between us will never last."

"And maybe you're wrong. Maybe the fact that we aren't in love is the reason that it will work. There won't be any unreasonable expectations. No emotional roller coaster."

"And that sounds good to you?"

He shrugged. "Do you have a better suggestion?"

"Yes. I think some space will be best for everyone."

"I don't agree. What would be best is if we became a family—a family that shares the same home as our children."

"And what happens—" She stopped herself just in time. She was going to utter, *What happens when you get bored*? Would he trade her in for a younger model? But she wasn't going there. It didn't matter because what Finn was proposing wasn't possible.

His gaze probed her. "Finish that statement."

"It's nothing."

"It was definitely something. And I want to know what it is." He moved closer to her.

His nearness sent her heart racing. It was hard to keep

her mind on the conversation. No man had a right to be so sexy. If only real life was like the movies and came with happily-ever-afters.

"Holly?"

"I honestly can't remember what I was going to say. But it's time I go back to New York."

Finn's eyes momentarily widened in surprise "What about the project?"

"The event is ready to go."

"You just said you had a problem with transportation."

"That…that's minor. I can deal with it from anywhere."

His gaze narrowed. "You're serious, aren't you?"

She settled her hands on her hips. "I am. You don't need me here. You can email me or phone, but you no longer need my presence here."

"Is there anything I can say to change your mind?"

There were so many things she wanted him to say. But she feared they were both too damaged—too cynical about life to be able to create a happily-ever-after.

And instead of trying and failing—of taking what they have and making it contentious, she'd rather part as friends. It'd be best for everyone, including the babies.

But finding herself a bit emotional, she didn't trust her voice. Instead, she averted her gaze and shook her head.

Finn sighed. "Fine. I'll call for the chopper."

"Really?" He was just going to let her walk out the door? It seemed too easy.

"It's what you want, isn't it?" He retrieved the phone.

"Yes, it is." She turned away and walked to the French doors. They were usually standing open, letting in the fresh air and sunshine, but not today. She stared off into the distant gray sky. Dark clouds scudded across it as rain began to fall.

She couldn't believe he was just going to let her walk away. A man who liked to control everything in his life surely couldn't live with just handing over his children with no strings attached.

In the background, she could hear the murmur of Finn's voice. He'd lowered it, but not before she caught the rumble in it. He wasn't happy—not at all. Well, that made two of them. But they'd have to make the best of the situation.

Her hand moved to her abdomen. It wouldn't be long now before she really started to show. She didn't even want to guess how big she'd get carrying not one but two babies. She had no doubt her figure would never be quite the same. But it would be worth it.

To be honest, she'd never thought of having children before. After her family had been ripped apart, she told herself she wasn't getting married or having children. She'd assured herself that life would be so much simpler when she only had herself to worry about.

Now she had two little ones counting on her to make all of the right decisions.

She turned, finding Finn with his back to her as he leaned against the desk. He certainly was different from Josh. Where Josh was a real charmer, Finn only gave a compliment when he truly meant it. Where Josh ran at the first sign of trouble, Finn was willing to stand by her. So why couldn't she give him a chance to prove that he truly was an exception?

He certainly was the most handsome man she'd laid her eyes on. Her gaze lingered on his golden hair that always seemed to be a bit scattered and made her long to run her fingers through it. And then there were his broad shoulders—shoulders that looked as though they could carry the weight of the world on them. She wondered how heavy a load he carried around.

Something told her he'd seen far too much in his young life. And she didn't want to add to his burden. That was never her intention. With time, she hoped he'd understand that she never meant to hurt him by turning down his suggestion of marriage.

Finn hung up the phone and turned to her. "We can't leave."

Surely she hadn't heard him correctly. "What do you mean we can't leave?"

"There's a storm moving in and with these high winds it's too dangerous to take up the chopper." His gaze met hers. "I'm sorry. I know how much you wanted off the island."

"So what are you saying? That we're stranded here?"

"Yes." He didn't look any happier about it than she did.

"What are we going to do?"

"You're going to wait here." He turned toward the door. "With Emilio and Maria away, I've got a lot of work to do before the storm. I won't get it all done tonight, but I can at least start."

"Wait for me. I want to help."

She rushed after him. There was no way she was planning to stand around and have him do all of the work. She knew her way around a toolbox and power tools. She could pull her own weight.

Hopefully this storm would pass by the island, leaving them unscathed. And then she'd be on her way home. She wasn't sure how much longer she could keep her common sense while around Finn.

Her gaze trailed down over Finn from his muscled arms to his trim waist and his firm backside. The blood heated in her veins. Enjoying each other's company didn't mean they had to make a formal commitment, right?

Wait. No. No. She couldn't let her desires override her logic. She jerked her gaze away from Finn. It had to be the pregnancy hormones that had her thinking these truly outlandish thoughts.

She was immune to Finn—about as immune as a bee to a field of wildflowers. She was in big trouble.

CHAPTER THIRTEEN

WHY WAS SHE fighting him?

The next day, Finn sighed as he stared blindly out the glass doors. No matter what he said to Holly, there was no reasoning with her. She was determined to have these babies on her own.

He knew that she wouldn't keep him from seeing them, but he also knew that visitation every other weekend was not enough. He would be a stranger to his own children—his only family. His hands clenched. That couldn't happen.

He'd never thought he'd be a part of a family again. And though he had worries about how well he'd measure up as a husband and father, he'd couldn't walk away. Why couldn't Holly understand that?

He didn't know how or when, but somehow he'd convince her that they were better parents together than apart. If only he knew how to get his point across to her—

The lights flickered, halting his thoughts. The power went completely out, shrouding the house in long shadows. After a night and day of rain, it had stopped, but the winds were starting to pick up again. And then the lights came back on.

Finn didn't like the looks of things outside—not one little bit. Normally there weren't big weather events at this time of the year, but every once in a while a late-season storm would make its way across the Atlantic. This just happened to be one of those times.

Finn rinsed a dinner plate and placed it in the dishwasher. Yes, to Holly's amazement, he did know his way around the kitchen. He was a man who preferred his privacy and he didn't have a regular household staff in New York, just a maid who came in a couple of times a week.

But here on the island, it was different. Maria and Emilio had a small house off in the distance. They lived here year-round. Maria looked after the house while Emilio took care of the grounds. They were as close to family as Finn had—until now.

He ran the dishcloth over the granite countertop before placing it next to the sink. Everything was clean and in its place. He wondered what Holly was up to. She'd been particularly quiet throughout dinner. He made his way to the study.

Though she wouldn't admit it, he could tell the storm had her on edge. He was concerned, too. The tide was much higher than normal and the wind was wicked. But this house had been built to withstand some of the harshest weather. They'd be safe here.

Now if only he could comfort Holly, but she resisted any attempt he made to get closer. He wondered what had happened for her to hide behind a defensive wall. It had to be something pretty bad. If only he could get her to open up to him.

He was in the hallway outside the study when the lights flickered and went out. This time they didn't come back on. He needed to check on Holly before he ventured outside to fire up the emergency generator.

He stepped into the study that was now long with shadows. He squinted, looking for her. "Holly, where are you?"

She stood up from behind one of the couches. "Over here."

"What in the world are you doing?"

"Looking for candles in this cabinet."

"There are no candles in here. I have some in the kitchen."

She followed him to the supply of candles. There were also flashlights and lanterns in the pantry. It was fully stocked in case of an emergency.

"Do you think we'll really need all of this?" She fingered

the packages of beef jerky and various other prepackaged foods.

"I hope not. The last I checked the weather radio, the storm was supposed to go south of us."

"And I think it's calming down outside. That has to be a good sign, doesn't it?"

When he glanced over at the hopefulness in her eyes, he didn't want to disappoint her. He wanted to be able to reassure her that everything would be fine, but something told him she'd already been lied to enough in her life. So he decided to change the subject.

He picked up a lantern. "I think this might be easier than the candles."

"Really?"

Was that a pout on her face? She wanted the candlelight? Was it possible there was a romantic side to her hidden somewhere beneath her practicality and cynicism?

Deciding it wouldn't hurt to indulge her, he retrieved some large candle jars. "Is this what you had in mind?"

She nodded. "But we won't need them, will we?"

Finn glanced outside. It was much darker than it normally would be at this time of the day. "Come on. I have a safe place for us to wait out the storm."

She didn't question him but rather she quietly followed him to the center of the house. He opened the door to a small room with reinforced walls and no windows.

"What is this?"

"A safe room. I know it's not very big, but trust me, it'll do the job. I had it specifically put in the house for this very reason." With a flashlight in hand, he started lighting the candles. "There. That's all of them." A loud bang echoed through the house. "Now, I'll go work on the generator."

Holly reached out, grasping his arm. "Please don't go outside."

"But I need to—"

"Stay safe. We've got everything we need right here."

"Holly, don't worry. This isn't my first storm."

"But it's mine. Promise me you won't go outside."

He stared into her big brown eyes and saw the fear reflected in them. It tore at his heart. He pulled her close until her cheek rested against his shoulder.

"Everything will be fine."

She pulled back in order to gaze into his eyes. "Promise me you won't go outside."

He couldn't deny her this. "Yes, I promise."

This time she squeezed him tight as though in relief.

Seconds later, Finn pulled away. "I think we'll need some more candles and I want to do one more walk through the house to make sure it's secure. I'll be back."

"I can come with you."

"No. Stay here and get comfortable. I'll be right back. I promise." He started for the door.

"Finn?"

He paused, hearing the fear in her voice. "Do you need something else?"

"Um, no. Just be careful."

"I will." Was it possible that through all of her defensiveness and need to assert her independence that she cared for him? The thought warmed a spot in his chest. But he didn't have time to dwell on this revelation. The winds were starting to howl.

He hurried back to the kitchen where he'd purposely forgotten the weather radio. He wanted to listen to it without Holly around. He didn't know much about pregnant women, but he knew enough to know stress would not be good for her.

The radio crackled. He adjusted it so he could make out most of the words. The eye of the storm had shifted. It was headed closer to them. And the winds were intensifying to hurricane strength. Finn's hands clenched tightly.

This was all his fault. He should have paid more attention to the weather instead of getting distracted with the babies and his plans for the future. Now, instead of worrying about what he'd be like as a father, he had to hope he'd get that chance. He knew how bad the tropical storms could get. He'd ridden one out in this very house a few years back. It was an experience he'd been hoping not to repeat.

With a sigh, he turned off the radio. He made the rounds. The house was as secure as he could make it. With the radio, satellite phone and a crate of candles and more water, he headed back to Holly.

"How is everything?" Her voice held a distinct thread of worry.

He closed the door and turned around to find a cozy setting awaiting him. There were blankets heaped on the floor and pillows lining the wall. With the soft glow of the candles, it swept him back in time—back to when his big brother was still alive. They were forever building blanket forts to their mother's frustration.

The memory of his mother and brother saddened him. Finn tried his best not to dwell on their absence from his life, but every now and then there would be a moment when a memory would drive home the fact that he was now all alone in this world.

"Finn, what is it?" Holly got to her feet and moved to him.

It wasn't until she pressed a hand to his arm that he was jarred from his thoughts. "Um, nothing. Everything is secure. It's started to rain."

"The storm's not going to miss us, is it?"

"I'm afraid not. But we'll be fine."

"With the door closed, it's amazing how quiet it is in here. I could almost pretend there isn't a big storm brewing outside."

He didn't want to keep talking about the weather. He didn't want her asking more questions, because the last thing he wanted to do was scare her with the word *hurricane*. After all, it wasn't even one yet, but there was a strong potential.

"I see you made the room comfortable."

She glanced around. "I hope you like it."

"I do." There was one thing about this arrangement—she couldn't get away from him. He had a feeling by the time the sun rose, things between them would be drastically different.

This was not working.

Holly wiggled around, trying to get comfortable. It wasn't the cushions so much as hearing the creaking of the house and wondering what was going on outside. Finn hadn't wanted to tell her so she hadn't pushed, but her best guess was that they were going to experience a hurricane. The thought sent a chill racing down her spine.

"Is something wrong?"

"Um, nothing."

She glanced across the short space to find Finn's handsome face illuminated in the candlelight. Why exactly had she insisted on the candles? Was she hoping there would be a bit of romance? Of course not. The soft light was comforting, was all.

His head lifted and his gaze met hers. "Do you need more cushions? Or a blanket?"

"Really, I'm fine." There was another loud creak of the house. "I... I'm just wondering what's going on outside. Should we go check?"

"No." His answer was fast and short. "I mean there could be broken glass and it's dark out there. We'll deal with it in the morning."

She swallowed hard. "You really think the windows have been blown out?"

"The shutters will protect them. Hopefully the house is holding its own."

"Maybe you should turn on the radio." Whatever the

weather people said couldn't be worse than what her imagination had conjured up.

"You know what I'd really like to do?" He didn't wait for her to respond. "How about we get to know each other better?"

"And how do you propose we do that?"

"How about a game of twenty questions? You can ask me anything you want and I have to be absolutely honest. In return, I get to ask you twenty questions and you have to be honest."

She wasn't so sure honesty right now would be such a good idea, especially if he asked if she cared about him. "I... I don't know."

"Oh, come on. Surely you have questions."

She did. She had lots of them, but she wasn't so sure she wanted to answer his in return. She didn't open up with many people. She told herself it was because she was introverted, but sometimes she wondered if it was more than that.

On this particular night everything felt surreal. Perhaps she could act outside her norm. "Okay, as long as I go first."

"Go for it. But remember you only get twenty questions so make them good ones."

CHAPTER FOURTEEN

HOLLY DIDN'T HAVE to think hard to come up with her first question. "Why did you look like you'd seen a ghost when you stepped in here?"

There was a pause as though Finn was figuring out how to answer her question. Was he thinking up a vague answer or would he really open up and give her a glimpse of the man beneath the business suits and intimidating reputation?

He glanced off into the shadows. "When I walked in here I was reminded of a time—long ago. My brother and I used to build blanket forts when we were kids. Especially in the winter when it was too cold or wet to go outside. My mother wasn't fond of them because we'd strip our beds."

Holly smiled, liking that he had a normal childhood with happy memories. She wondered why he kept them hidden. In all the time she'd been around him, she could count on one hand the number of times he spoke of his family. But she didn't say a word because she didn't want to interrupt him—she found herself wanting to learn everything she could about him.

"I remember there was this one Christmas where we'd built our biggest fort. But it was dark in there and my brother wanted to teach me to play cards. My mother would have been horrified that her proper young men were playing cards—it made it all the more fun. We tried a flashlight but it didn't have enough light. So my brother got an idea of where to get some lights."

Holly could tell by the gleam in Finn's eyes that mischief had been afoot. He and his brother must have been a handful. Would her twins be just as ornery? Her hand moved to her stomach. She had a feeling they would be and that she'd love every minute of it. She might even join them in their fort.

"While my parents were out at the Mistletoe Ball and the sitter was watching a movie in the family room, we took a string of white lights off the Christmas tree."

Holly gasped. "You didn't."

Finn nodded. "My brother assured me it was just one strand. There were plenty of other lights on the tree. After all, it was a big tree. So we strung the lights back and forth inside our fort. It gave it a nice glow, enough so that we could see the cards. There was just one problem."

"You got caught?"

He shook his head. "Not at first. The problem was my brother for all of his boasting had no clue how to play cards. So we ended up playing Go Fish."

Holly couldn't help but laugh, imagining those two little boys. "I bet you kept your parents on their toes."

"I suppose we did—for a while anyway." The smile slipped from his face and she wanted to put it back there. He was so handsome when he smiled.

"So what happened with the lights?"

"Well, when my parents got home, my mother called us down to the living room. It seems my father tried to fix the lights that were out on the lower part of the tree, but he soon found they were missing. My mother wanted to know if we knew anything about it. I looked at my brother and he looked at me. Then we both shrugged. We tried to assure her the tree looked good, but she wasn't buying any of it. My mother didn't have to look very long to find the lights. As I recall, we were grounded for a week. My father had the task of putting the lights back on the tree with all of the ornaments and ribbon still on it. He was not happy at all."

"I wouldn't think he would be."

"Okay. So now it's my turn. Let's see. Where did you grow up?"

She gave him a funny look. "Seriously, that's what you want to know?"

He shrugged. "Sure. Why not?"

"I grew up in Queens. A long way from your Upper East Side home."

"Not that far."

"Maybe not by train but it is by lifestyle." When Finn glanced away, she realized how that sounded. She just wasn't good at thinking about her family and the way things used to be so she always searched for a diversion.

"It's my turn." She thought for a moment and then asked, "Okay, what's your favorite color?"

He sent her a look of disbelief. "Are you serious?"

"Sure. Why wouldn't I be?"

"It's just that I thought these were questions to get to know each other. I don't know how my favorite color has much to do with anything."

"I'll tell you once you spit it out."

He sighed. "Green. Hunter green. Now why was that so important to you?"

"Are you sure it isn't money green?" He rolled his eyes and smiled at her before she continued. "It's important to me because I need a color to paint the babies' bedroom."

"Oh. I hadn't thought of that. Then I get to ask you what your favorite color is."

"Purple. A deep purple."

"Sounds like our children are going to have interesting bedrooms with purple and green walls."

Holly paused and thought about it for a minute. "I think we can make it work."

"Are you serious?"

"Very. Think about green foliage with purple skies. A palm tree with a monkey or two or three. And perhaps a bunch of bananas here and there for a splash of yellow."

His eyes widened. "How did you do that?"

"Do what?"

"Come up with that mural off the top of your head?"

She shrugged. "I don't know. It just sounded fun and like something our children might enjoy."

"I think you're right. I'll have the painters get started on it right away."

"Whoa! Slow down. I don't even know where we'll be living by the time these babies are born." When the smile slipped from his face, she knew it was time for a new question. "Why do you always leave New York at Christmastime? No, scratch that. I know that answer. I guess my real question is why do you hate Christmas?"

He frowned. "So now you're going for the really hard questions, huh? No, what's your middle name? Or what's your favorite food?"

She shrugged. "I just can't imagine hating Christmas. It's the season of hope."

There was a faraway look in his eyes. "My mother, she used to love it, too. She would deck out our house the day after Thanksgiving. It was a tradition. And it wasn't just her. The whole family took part, pulling the boxes of decorations out of the attic while Christmas carols played in the background. After we hung the outside lights, my mother would whip up hot chocolate with those little marshmallows."

"So you don't like it anymore because it reminds you of her?"

Finn frowned. "You don't get to ask another question yet. Besides, I wasn't finished with my answer."

"Oh. Sorry."

"Now that my family isn't around, I don't see any point in celebrating. I'll never get any of those moments back. When I'm here, I don't have to be surrounded by those memories or be reminded of what I lost."

There was more to that story, but she had to figure out the right question to get him to open up more. But how deep would he let her dig into his life? She had no idea. But if she didn't try to break through some of the protective layers that he had surrounding him, how in the world would they ever coparent? How would she ever be able to answer her children's questions about their father?

She didn't want to just ignore her kids' inquiries like her mother had done with her. Initially when her father had left, she'd been so confused. She thought it was something she'd done or not done. She didn't understand because to her naive thinking, things had been good. Then one day he packed his bags and walked out the door. Her mother refused to fill in the missing pieces. It was really hard for a ten-year-old to understand how her family had splintered apart overnight.

Finn cleared his throat. "Okay, next question. Do your parents still live in Queens?"

"Yes, however right now my mother's visiting my aunt in Florida. And my father moved to Brooklyn."

Finn's brow arched. "So they're divorced?"

"You already had your question, now it's my turn." Finn frowned but signaled with his hand for her to proceed, so she continued. "What happened to your brother?"

Finn's hands flexed. "He died."

She knew there had to be so much more to it. But she didn't push. If Finn was going to let down his guard, it had to be his choice, and pushing him would only keep him on the defensive.

And so she quietly waited. Either he expanded on his answer or he asked her another question. She would make peace with whatever he decided.

"My brother was the star of the family. He got top marks in school. He was on every sports team. And he shadowed my father on the weekends at the office. He was like my father in so many ways."

"And what about you?"

"I was a couple of years younger. I wasn't the Lockwood heir and so my father didn't have much time for me. I got the occasional clap on the back for my top marks, but then my father would turn his attention to my brother. For the most part, it didn't bother me. It was easier being forgotten than being expected to be perfect. My brother didn't have it easy. The pressure my father put on him to excel at everything was enormous."

Holly didn't care what Finn said, to be forgotten by a parent or easily dismissed hurt deeply. She knew all about it when her father left them to start his own family with his mistress, now wife number two.

But this wasn't her story, it was Finn's. And she knew it didn't have a happy ending, but she didn't know the details. Perhaps if she'd dug deeper on the internet, she might have learned how Finn's family splintered apart, but she'd rather hear it all from him.

"Everything was fine until my brother's grades started to fall and he began making mistakes on the football field. My father was irate. He blamed it on my brother being a teenager and being distracted by girls. My brother didn't even have a girlfriend at that point. He was too shy around them."

Holly tried to decide if that was true of Finn, as well. Somehow she had a hard time imagining this larger-than-life man being shy. Perhaps he could be purposely distant, but she couldn't imagine him being nervous around a woman.

"My brother, he started to tire easily. It progressed to the point where my mother took him to the doctor. It all snowballed from there. Tests and treatments became the sole focus of the whole house. Christmas that year was forgotten."

"How about you?" He didn't say it, but she got the feeling with so much on the line that Finn got lost in the shuffle.

He frowned at her, but it was the pain in his eyes that dug at her. "I didn't have any right to feel forgotten. My brother was fighting for his life."

She lowered her voice. "But it had to be tough for you with everyone running around looking after your brother. No one would blame you for feeling forgotten."

"I would blame me. I was selfish." His voice was gravelly with emotion. "And I had no right—no right to want presents on Christmas—no right to grow angry with my parents for not having time for me."

Her heart ached for him. "Of course you would want Christmas with all of its trimmings. Your life was spinning out of control and you wanted to cling to what you knew—what would make your life feel normal again."

"Aren't you listening? My brother was dying and I was sitting around feeling sorry for myself because I couldn't have some stupid toys under the Christmas tree. What kind of a person does that make me?"

"A real flesh-and-blood person who isn't perfect. But here's a news flash for you. None of us are—perfect that is. We just have to make the best of what we've been given."

He shook his head, blinking repeatedly. "I'm worse than most. I'm selfish and thoughtless. *Uncaring* is the word my mother threw at me." He swiped at his eyes. "And she was right. My brother deserved a better sibling than I'd turned out to be."

Holly placed her hand atop his before lacing their fingers together. A tingling sensation rushed from their clasped hands, up her arm and settled in her chest. It gave her the strength she needed to keep going—to keep trying to help this man who was in such pain.

"Did you ever think that you were just a kid in a truly horrific situation? Your big brother—the person you looked up to—your best friend—was sick, dying and there was nothing you could do for him. That's a lot to deal with as an adult, but as a child you must have felt utterly helpless. Not knowing what to do with the onslaught of emotions, you pushed them aside. Your brother's situation was totally out of your control. Instead you focused on trying to take control of your life."

Finn's wounded gaze searched hers. "You're just saying that to make me feel better."

"I'm saying it because it's what I believe." She freed her hand from his in order to gently caress his jaw. "Finn, you're a good man with a big heart—"

"I'm not. I'm selfish."

"Is that what your mother told you?"

"No." His head lowered. There was a slight pause as though he was lost in his own memories. "It's what my father told me."

"He was wrong." She placed a fingertip beneath Finn's chin and lifted until they were eye to eye. "He was very wrong. You have the biggest, most generous heart of anyone I know."

"Obviously you don't know me very well." His voice was barely more than a whisper.

"Look at how much you do for others. The Santa Project is a prime example. And you're a generous boss with an amazing benefits package for your employees—"

"That isn't what I meant. My father...he told me that I should have been the one in the hospital bed, not my brother." Holly gasped. Finn kept talking as though oblivious to her shocked reaction. "He was right. My brother was the golden boy. He was everything my parents could want. Derek and I were quite different."

Tears slipped down her cheeks. It was horrific that his father would spew such mean and hurtful things, but the fact that Finn believed them and still did to this day tore her up inside. How in the world did she make him see what a difference he continued to make in others' lives?

And then a thought occurred to her. She pulled his hand over to her slightly rounded abdomen. "This is the reason you're still here. You have a future. You have two little ones coming into this world that you can lavish with love and let them know how important each of them are to you. You can make sure they know that you don't have a favorite because they are equally important in your heart."

"What…what if I end up like my father and hurt our children?"

"You won't. The fact you're so worried about it proves my point."

His gaze searched hers. "Do you really believe that? You think I can be a good father?"

"I do." Her voice held a note of conviction. "Just follow your heart. It's a good, strong heart. It won't lead you astray."

"No one ever said anything like this to me. I… I just hope I don't let you down."

"You won't. I have faith in you."

His gaze dipped to her lips. She could read his thoughts and she wanted him too. Not waiting for him, she leaned forward, pressing her lips to his.

At first, he didn't move. Was he that surprised by her action? Didn't he know how much she wanted him? Needed him?

As his lips slowly moved beneath hers, she'd never felt so close to anyone in her life. It was though his words had touched her heart. He'd opened up and let her in. That was a beginning.

Her hands wound around his neck. He tasted sweet like the fresh batch of Christmas cookies that she'd left on a plate in the kitchen. She was definitely going to have to make more of those.

As their kiss deepened, her fingers combed through his hair. A moan rose in the back of her throat. She'd never been kissed so thoroughly. Her whole body tingled clear down to her toes.

Right now though, she didn't want anything but his arms around her as they sank down into the nest of blankets and pillows. While the storm raged outside, desire raged inside her.

CHAPTER FIFTEEN

IT COULD BE BETTER.

But it could have been so much worse.

The next morning, Finn returned to the safe room after a preliminary survey of the storm damage. He glanced down at the cocoon of blankets and pillows to find Holly awake and getting to her feet. With her hair slightly mussed up and her lips still rosy from a night of kissing, she'd never looked more beautiful.

She blushed. "What are you looking at?" She ran a hand over her hair. "I must be a mess."

"No. Actually you look amazing."

"You're just saying that because you want something from me."

He hadn't said it for any reason other than he meant it. However, now that she'd planted the idea into his head, perhaps now was as good a time as any to tell her what he had on his mind. He'd stared into the dark long after she'd fallen asleep the night before. He'd thought long and hard about where they went from here.

But now as she smiled up at him, his attention strayed to her soft, plump lips. "You're right, there is something I want." He reached out and pulled her close. "This."

Without giving her a chance to react, he leaned in and pressed his lips to hers. Her kisses were sweet as nectar and he knew he'd never ever tire of them. He pulled her closer, deepening the kiss. He needed to make sure that last night hadn't just been a figment of his imagination.

And now he had his proof. The chemistry between them was most definitely real. It was all the more reason to follow through with his plan—his duty.

When at last he let her go, she smiled up at him. "What was that about?"

"Just making sure you aren't a dream."

"I'm most definitely real and so was that storm last night. So, um, how bad is the damage?" She turned and started to collect the blankets.

"There's a lot of debris on the beach. It'll take a while until this place looks like it once did, but other than a few minor things, the house held its own."

"That's wonderful. How long until we have power?"

"I'm hoping not long. I plan to work on that first." They were getting off topic.

"Before I let you go, I do believe we got distracted last night before I could ask my next question."

"Hmm... I don't recall this." She sent him a teasing smile.

"Convenient memory is more like it."

"Okay. What's your question?"

Now that it was time to put his marriage plan in action, he had doubts—lots of them. What if she wanted more than he could offer? What if she wanted a traditional marriage with promises of love?

"Finn? What is it?"

"Will you marry me?"

Surprise reflected in her eyes. "We already had this conversation. It won't work."

"Just hear me out. It won't be a traditional marriage, but that doesn't mean we can't make it work. After all, we're friends—or I'd like to think we are." She nodded in agreement and he continued. "And we know we're good together in other areas."

Pink tinged her cheeks. "So this would be like a business arrangement?"

"Not exactly. It'll be what we make of it. So what do you say?"

She returned to folding a blanket. "We don't have to be

married to be a family. I still believe we'll all be happier if you have your life and I have my own."

A frown pulled at his lips. This wasn't the way it had played out in his imagination. In his mind, she'd jumped at the offer. If she was waiting for something more—something heartfelt—she'd be waiting a very long time.

There had to be a way to turn this around. The stakes were much too high for him to fold his hand and walk away. He needed to be close to his children—

"Stop." Her voice interrupted the flow of his thoughts.

"Stop what?"

"Wondering how you can get me to say yes. You can't. I told you before that I didn't want to get married. That hasn't changed."

But the part she'd forgotten was that he was a man used to getting his way. When he set his sights on something, nothing stood in his way. He would overcome her hesitation about them becoming a full-fledged family, no matter what it took.

He wanted to be a full-time father to his kids and do all the things his father had been too busy to do with him. He would make time for both of his children. He wouldn't demean one while building up the other. Or at least he would try his darnedest to be a fair and loving parent.

And that was where Holly came into the plan. She would be there to watch over things—to keep the peace and harmony in the family. He knew already that she wouldn't hesitate to call him out on the carpet if he started to mess up where the kids were concerned.

He needed that reassurance—Holly's guidance. There was no way that he was going to let her go. But could he give her his heart?

Everyone he'd ever loved or thought that he'd loved, he'd lost. He couldn't go through that again. He couldn't have Holly walk out on him. It was best that they go into this marriage as friends with benefits as well as parents to their twins. Emotions were overrated.

The storm had made a real mess of things.

And Holly found herself thankful for the distraction. She moved around the living room where one of the floor-to-ceiling window panes had been broken when a shutter had been torn off its hinge. There was a mess of shattered glass everywhere.

So while Finn worked on restoring the power to the house, she worked on making the living room inhabitable again. But as the winds whipped through the room, she knew that as soon as Finn was free, she needed his help to put plywood over the window. But for now she was happy for the solitude.

If she didn't know better, she'd swear she dreamed up that marriage proposal. Finn Lockwood proposed to little old her. She smiled. He had no idea how tempted she was to accept his proposal. She'd always envied her friends getting married...until a few years down the road when some of them were going through a nasty divorce.

No, she couldn't—she wouldn't set herself up to get hurt. And now it wasn't just her but her kids that would be hurt when the marriage fell apart. She was right in turning him down. She just had to stick to her resolve. Everyone would be better off because of it.

So then why didn't she feel good about her decision? Why did she feel as though she'd turned down the best offer in her entire life?

It wasn't like she was madly in love with him. Was she?

Oh, no. It was true.

She loved Finn Lockwood.

When exactly had that happened?

She wasn't quite sure.

Though the knowledge frightened her, she couldn't deny it. What did she do now?

"Holly?"

She jumped. Her other hand, holding some of the broken glass, automatically clenched. Pain sliced through her fingers and she gasped. She released her grip, letting the glass fall back to the hardwood floor.

Finn rushed to her side. "I'm sorry. I didn't mean to startle you." He gently took her hand in his to examine it. "You've cut yourself. Let's get you out of here."

"I... I'll be fine."

"We'll see about that." He led her to the bathroom and stuck her hand under the faucet. "What were you doing in there?"

"Cleaning up. What did you think?"

"You should have waited. I would have done it. Or I would have flown in a cleaning crew. But I never expected you to do it, not in your condition."

"My condition? You make it sound like I've got some sort of disease instead of being pregnant with two beautiful babies."

"That wasn't my intent."

She knew that. She was just being touchy because... because he'd gotten past all of her defenses. He'd gotten her to fall in love with him and she'd never felt more vulnerable.

"What had you so distracted when I walked in?" Finn's gaze met hers as he dabbed a soapy washcloth to her fingers and palm.

"It was nothing." Nothing that she was ready to share. Once she did, he'd reason away her hesitation to get further involved with him.

"It had to be something if it had you so distracted that you didn't even hear me enter the room. Were you reconsidering my proposal?"

He couldn't keep proposing to her. It was dangerous. One of these days he might catch her in a weak moment and she might say yes. It might have a happy beginning but it was the ending that worried her.

She knew how to put an end to it. She caught and held his gaze. Her heart *thump-thumped* as she swallowed hard, working up the courage to get the words out. "Do you love me?"

His mouth opened, but just as quickly he pressed his lips together. He didn't love her. Her heart pinched. In that moment she realized that she'd wanted him to say yes. She wanted him to say that he was absolutely crazy in love with her. Inwardly, she groaned. What was happening to her? She was the skeptic—the person who didn't believe in happily-ever-afters.

"We don't have to love each other to make a good marriage." He reached out to her, gripping her elbows and pulling her to him. "This will work. Trust me."

She wanted to say that she couldn't marry someone who didn't love her, but she didn't trust herself mentioning the L-word. "I do trust you. But we're better off as friends."

He sighed. "What I need is a wife and a mother for my children."

"You know what they say, two out of three isn't bad."

His brows scrunched together as though not following her comment.

She gazed into his eyes, trying to ignore the pain she saw reflected there. "We're friends or at least I'd like to think we are." He nodded in agreement and she continued. "And I'm the mother of your children. That's two things. But I just can't be your wife. I won't agree to something that in the end will hurt everyone. You've already experienced more than enough pain in your life. I won't add to it. Someday you'll find the right woman."

"What if I'm looking at her?"

She glanced away. "Now that the storm's over, I think I should get back to New York."

Finn dabbed antibiotic cream on her nicks and cuts before adding a couple of bandages. Without another word, he started cleaning up the mess in the bathroom. Fine. If he wanted to act this way, so could she.

She walked away, but inside her heart felt as though it'd been broken in two. Why did life have to be so difficult? Her vision blurred with unshed tears, but she blinked them away.

If only she could be like other people and believe in the impossible, then she could jump into his arms—she could be content with the present and not worry about the future.

CHAPTER SIXTEEN

Two busy days had now passed since the tropical storm. Finn had done everything in his power to put the house back to normal. The physical labor had been exactly what he needed to work out his frustrations.

Toward the end of the day, Emilio phoned to say that the storm was between them and he couldn't get a flight out of Florida yet. Finn told him not to worry, he had everything under control and that Emilio should enjoy his new grandchild.

"Do you want some more to eat?" Holly's voice drew him from his thoughts.

Finn glanced down at his empty dinner plate. She'd made spaghetti and meatballs. He'd had some jar sauce and frozen meatballs on hand. He didn't always want someone to cook for him—sometimes he liked the solitude. So he made sure to keep simple things on hand that he could make for himself.

"Thanks. It was good but I'm full."

"There's a lot of leftovers. I guess I'm not so good with portions. I'll put them in the fridge in case you get hungry later. I know how hard you worked today. I'm sorry I wasn't any help."

"You have those babies to care for now. Besides, you cooked. That was a huge help."

She sent him a look that said she didn't believe him, but she wasn't going to argue. "I'll just clean this up."

He got to his feet. "Let me help."

She shook her head. "You rest. I've got this."

"But I want to help. And I'd like to make a pot of coffee. Do you want some?"

"I can't have any now that I'm pregnant."

"That's right. I forgot. But don't worry. I plan to do lots of reading. I'll catch on to all of this pregnancy stuff. Well, come on. The kitchen isn't going to clean itself."

When he entered the kitchen, he smiled. For a woman who was utterly organized in the office, he never expected her skills in the kitchen to be so, um, chaotic.

Normally such a mess would have put him on edge, but this one had the opposite effect on him. He found himself relaxing a bit knowing she was human with flaws and all. Maybe she wouldn't expect him to be the perfect dad. Maybe she would be understanding about his shortcomings.

Holly insisted on cleaning off the dishes while he placed them in the dishwasher. In the background, the coffeemaker hissed and sputtered. They worked in silence. Together they had everything cleaned up in no time.

"There. That's it." Holly closed the fridge with the leftovers safely inside.

After filling a coffee mug, he turned to Holly. "Come with me. I think we need to talk some more."

She crossed her arms. "If this is about your marriage proposal, there's nothing left to say except when can I catch a flight back to New York?"

He'd already anticipated this and had a solution. "Talk with me while I drink my coffee and then I'll go check on the helipad."

"Do you think it's damaged?"

Luckily the helicopter had been on the big island for routine maintenance when the storm struck. It was unharmed. However, with so many other things that had snagged his immediate concern, he hadn't checked on the helipad. Anything could have happened during that storm, but his gut was telling him that if the house was in pretty good condition then the helipad wouldn't be so bad off.

"Don't worry. The storm wasn't nearly as bad as it could have been."

The worry lines marring Holly's face eased a bit. With a cup of coffee in one hand and a glass of water in the other for her, he followed Holly to his office. Luckily the windows had held in here.

"Why don't we sit on the couch?"

While she took a seat, he dimmed the lights and turned on some sexy jazz music. Cozy and relaxing. He liked it this way. And then he sat down next to Holly.

Her gaze narrowed in on him. "What are you up to?"

He held up his palms. "Nothing. I swear. This is how I like to unwind in the evenings."

The look in her eyes said that she didn't believe him.

"Listen, I'll sit on this end of the couch and you can stay at the other end. Will that work?"

She nodded. "I don't know why you'd have to unwind on a beautiful island like this—well, it's normally beautiful. Will you be able to get it back to normal?"

She was avoiding talking about them and their future. It was as though she was hoping he'd forget what he wanted to talk to her about. That was never going to happen.

Still needing time to figure out exactly how to handle this very sensitive situation, he'd come up with a way to give them both some time. "I have a proposition for you—"

"If this is about getting married—"

"Just hear me out." When she remained silent, he turned on the couch so that he could look at her. "Can I be honest with you?"

"Of course. I'd hope you wouldn't even have to ask the question. I'd like to think that you're always honest—but I know that isn't true for most people." Her voice trailed off as she glanced down at her clenched hands.

She'd been betrayed? Anger pumped through his veins. Was it some guy that she'd loved? How could anyone lie to her and hurt her so deeply? The thought was inconceivable until he realized how he'd unintentionally hurt those that were closest to him. And he realized that if he wasn't careful and kept her at a safe distance that he would most likely hurt her, too. The fire and rage went out of him.

Still, he had to know what had cost Holly her ability to trust in others. "What happened?"

Her gaze lifted to meet his. "What makes you think something happened?"

"I think it's obvious. I shared my past with you. It's your turn. What's your story?"

She sighed. "It's boring and will probably sound silly to you because it's nothing as horrific as what you went through with your brother."

"I'll be the judge of that. But if it hurt you, I highly doubt that it's silly. Far from it."

Her eyes widened. "You're really interested, aren't you?"

"Of course I am. Everything about you interests me."

Her cheeks grew rosy as she glanced away. "My early childhood was happy and for all I knew, normal. My father worked—a lot. But my mother was there. We did all sorts of things together from baking to shopping to going to the park. I didn't have any complaints. Well, I did want a little brother or sister, but my mother always had an excuse of why it was best with just the three of us. I never did figure out if she truly wanted another baby and couldn't get pregnant or if she knew in her gut that her marriage was in trouble and didn't want to put another child in the middle of it."

"Or maybe she was just very happy with the child she already had." He hoped that was the right thing to say. He wasn't experienced with comforting words.

"Anyway when I was ten, my father stopped coming home. At first, my mother brushed off my questions, telling me that he was on an extended business trip. But at night, when she thought I was sleeping, I could hear her crying in her room. I knew something was seriously wrong. I started to wonder if my father had died. So I asked her and that's when she broke down and told me that he left us to start a new family. Then he appeared one day and, with barely a word, he packed his things and left."

"I'm so sorry." Finn moved closer to Holly. Not knowing what words to say at this point, he reached out, taking her hand into his own.

"My mother, she didn't cope well with my father being gone. She slipped into depression to the point where I got myself up and dressed in the morning for school. I cooked and cleaned up what I could. I even read to my mother, like she used to do with me when I was little. I needed her to get better, because I needed her since I didn't have anyone else."

"That must have been so hard for you. Your father…was he around at all?"

Holly shook her head. "I didn't know it then, but later I learned my stepmother was already pregnant with Suzie. My father had moved on without even waiting for the divorce. He had a new family and he'd forgotten about us…about me."

Finn's body tensed. He knew what it was like to be forgotten by a parent. But at least his parents had a really good excuse, at first it was because his brother was sick and then they'd been lost in their own grief. But Holly's father, he didn't have that excuse. Finn disliked the man intensely and he hadn't even met him.

"When the divorce was finalized, my father got visitation. Every other weekend, I went to stay with him and his new family. Every time my parents came face-to-face it was like a world war had erupted. My mother would grouch to me about my father and in turn, my father would bad-mouth my mother. It was awful." She visibly shuddered. "No child should ever be a pawn between their parents."

"I agree." Finn hoped that was the right thing to say. Just for good measure, he squeezed Holly's hand, hoping she'd know that he really did care even if he didn't have all of the right words.

"I don't want any of that for our children. I don't want them to be pawns between us."

"They won't. I swear it. No matter what happens between us, we'll put the kids first. We both learned that lesson first-hand. But will you do something for me?"

"What's that?"

His heart pounded in his chest. He didn't know what he'd do if she turned him down. "Would you give us a chance?"

Her fine brows gathered. "What sort of chance?"

That was the catch. He wasn't quite sure what he was asking of her—or of himself. Returning to New York with the holiday season in full swing twisted his insides into a knot. The reminders of what he'd lost would be everywhere. But it was where Holly and the babies would be.

He stared deep into her eyes. His heart pounded. And yet within her gaze, he found the strength he needed to make this offer—a chance to build the family his children deserved.

He swallowed hard. "I'd like to see where this thing between us leads. Give me until the New Year—you know, with us working closely together. That will give Clara time for an extended honeymoon and to settle into married life. And we'll have time to let down our guards and really get to know each other."

"I thought that's what we've been doing."

"But as fast as you let down one wall, I feel like you're building another one."

She worried her bottom lip. "Perhaps you're right. It's been a very long time since I've been able to count on some-one. It might take me a bit of time to get it right." She eyed him up. "But I have something I need you to do in return."

"Name it."

"Be honest with me. Even if you don't think that I'll like it, just tell me. I couldn't stand to be blindsided like my mother. And there was a guy I got serious with while I was getting my degree. Long story short, he lied to me about his gambling addiction and then he stole from me to cover his debts."

"Wow. You haven't had it easy."

She shrugged. "Let's just say I have my reasons to be cautious."

"I promise I won't lie to you." She meant too much to him to hurt her. "Now, I need to go check on the helipad."

"What about the recommendation?" When he sent her a puzzled look, she added, "You know, for that other job?"

"You still want to leave? Even though we agreed to see where this leads us?"

"What if it leads nowhere? It'll be best if you don't have to see me every day."

His back teeth ground together. Just the thought of her no longer being in his life tied his insides up in a knot. For so long, he'd sentenced himself to a solitary life. And now he couldn't imagine his life without Holly in it.

"Let's not worry about the future. We can take this one day at a time." It was about all he could manage at this point.

"It's a deal." And then she did something he hadn't expected. She held her hand out to him to shake on it.

It was as though she was making this arrangement something much more distant and methodical than what he had in mind. He slipped his hand into hers. As her fingertips grazed over his palm, the most delicious sensations pulsed up his arm, reminding him that they'd passed the business associates part of their relationship a long time ago.

He needed to give Holly something else to think about. Without giving himself the time to think of all the reasons that his next actions were a bad idea, he tightened his fingers around her hand and pulled her to him.

Her eyes widened as he lowered his head and caught her

lips with his own—her sweet, sweet lips. He didn't care how many times he kissed her, it wouldn't be enough.

And then not wanting to give her a reason to hide behind another defensive wall, he pulled away. Her eyes had darkened. Was that confusion? No. What he was seeing reflected in her eyes was desire. A smile tugged at his lips. His work was done here.

He got to his feet. "I'll go check on the helipad."

With a flashlight in hand, he made his way along the path to the helipad. He had no idea what to expect when he got there. If it was clear, there was no reason Holly couldn't leave in the morning. The thought gutted him.

He'd just reached the head of the path when the rays of his flashlight skimmed over the helipad. As though fate was on his side, there were a couple of downed trees, making the landing zone inaccessible. But luckily it didn't appear they'd done any permanent damage—at least nothing to make the helipad inoperable.

It was much too dark now, but in the morning he'd have to get the chain saw out here. He imagined it'd be at least a couple of days to get this stuff cleared. It was time that he could use to sort things out with Holly.

CHAPTER SEVENTEEN

A PAIN TORE through Holly's side.

The plates holding cold-cut sandwiches clattered onto the table. Holly pressed a hand to her waistline, willing the throbbing to subside. She rubbed the area, surprised by how much she was actually showing. But with twins on board, she figured that was to be expected. Thankfully when they'd visited the big island, she'd picked up some new, roomy clothes. They were all she wore now.

The discomfort ebbed away. Everything would be okay. It had to be. She was in the house alone. Finn had gone to the helipad first thing that morning to clear the debris. He didn't say exactly how bad it was, but she had a feeling he had a lot of work ahead of him if it was anything like the beach area.

She'd offered to help, but he'd stubbornly refused. So she set about cleaning the patio and washing it down so that it was usable again. All in all, they'd fared really well.

In a minute or so the discomfort passed. Realizing she might have overreacted, she shrugged it off and moved to the deck. She loved that Finn had installed a large bell. It could be rung in the case of an emergency or to call people for lunch, as she was about to do.

She wrapped her fingers around the weathered rope and pulled. The bell rang out.

Clang-clang. Clang-clang.

"Lunch!" She didn't know if he'd hear her, but hopefully he'd heard the bell.

She turned back to go inside the house to finish setting the table for lunch. She smiled, wondering if this was what it felt like to be a part of a couple. She knew they weren't a real couple, but they were working together. And she was happy—truly happy for the first time in a long while. She glanced around the island. Wouldn't it be nice to stay here until the babies were born?

A dreamy sigh escaped her lips. If only that could happen, but the realistic part of her knew it wasn't a possibility. Soon enough this fantasy would be over and she'd be back in New York, settling into a new job and trying to figure out how to juggle a job and newborns.

One day at a time. I have months until these little ones make their grand entrance.

At last, having the table set, she heard footsteps outside. Finn had heard her. Her heart beat a little faster, knowing she'd get to spend some time with him. Sure it was lunch, but he'd been gone all morning. She'd started to miss him.

Quit being ridiculous. You're acting like a teenager with a huge crush.

No. It's even worse. I'm a grown woman who is falling more in love with my babies' daddy with each passing day.

"I heard the bell. Is it time to eat?" He hustled through the doorway in his stocking feet. "I'm starved."

She glanced up to find Finn standing there in nothing but his jeans and socks. She had no idea what had happened to his shirt, but she heartily approved of his attire. Her gaze zeroed in on the tanned muscles of his shoulders and then slid down to his well-defined pecs and six-pack abs. Wow! She swallowed hard. Who knew hard work could look so good on a man?

His eyes twinkled when he smiled. "Is something wrong?"

Wrong? Absolutely nothing. Nothing at all.

"Um…no. I… I made up some sandwiches." Her face felt as though it was on fire. "The food, it's on the table. If you want to clean up a bit, we can eat." Realizing that she hadn't put out any refreshments, she asked, "What would you like to drink?"

"Water is good. Ice cold."

It did sound particularly good at the moment. "You got it."

She rushed around, getting a couple of big glasses and filling them with ice. Right about now she just wanted to climb in the freezer to cool off. It wasn't like he was the first guy she'd seen with his shirt off. Why in the world was she overreacting?

Get a grip, Holly.

She placed the glasses on the table and then decided something was missing. But what? She glanced around the kitchen, looking for something to dress up the table and then she spotted the colorful blooms she'd picked that morning. They were in a small vase on the counter. Their orange, yellow and pink petals would add a nice splash to the white tablecloth.

A pain shot through her left side again. Immediately her hand pressed to her side as she gripped the back of a chair with her other hand.

"What's the matter?" Finn's concerned voice filled the room, followed by his rapid footsteps.

She didn't want to worry him. "It's nothing."

"It's something. Tell me."

"It's the second time I've had a pain in my side."

"Pain?" His arm wrapped around her as he helped her sit down. "Is it the babies?"

"I... I don't know." She looked up at him, hoping to see reassurance in his eyes. Instead his worry reflected back at her. "It's gone now."

"You're sure?"

She nodded. "Let's eat."

"I think you need to see a doctor. The sooner, the better." He pulled out his cell phone. "In fact, I'm going to call the doctor now."

"What? But you can't. Honest, it's gone."

"I'll feel better once I hear it from someone who has experience in these matters."

A short time later, after Finn had gotten through to the doctor who'd examined her on the big island, Finn had relinquished the phone to Holly. She'd answered the doctor's questions and then breathed a sigh of relief.

When she returned the phone to Finn, his brow was knit into a worried line. She was touched that he cared so much. It just made her care about him all the more.

"Well, what did he say?"

"That without any other symptoms it sounds like growing pains. But it was hard for him to diagnose me over the phone. The only reason he did was because I told him we were stranded on the island due to the storm."

The stiff line of Finn's shoulders eased. "He doesn't think it's anything urgent?"

She shrugged. "He said I needed to make an appointment and see my OB/GYN as soon as possible just to be sure."

"Then that's what we'll do. We'll be out of here by this evening."

"What? But we can't. What about the trees and stuff at the helipad?"

"I just got the motivation I need to clear it. So you call your doctor and see if they can squeeze you in for tomorrow, and I'll call my pilot and have him fuel up the jet. We'll leave tonight."

"But you don't have to go. I know you don't want to be in New York for the holidays."

"That was before."

"Before what?"

"You know."

Her gaze narrowed in on him. "No, I don't know. Tell me."

"Before you and me...before the babies. We agreed we

were going to give this thing a go and this is me doing my part. You haven't changed your mind, have you?"

He cared enough to spend the holidays with her in the city. Her heart leaped for joy. Okay, so she shouldn't get too excited. She knew in the long run the odds were against them, but Christmas was the season of hope.

Things were looking up.

Finn stared out the back of the limo as they inched their way through the snarled Manhattan traffic. He could at last breathe a lot easier now. The babies and their mother were healthy. It was indeed growing pains. The doctor told them to expect more along the way.

Signs of Christmas were everywhere from the decorated storefronts to the large ornaments hung from the lampposts. As he stared out the window, he saw Santa ringing a bell next to his red kettle. It made Finn wish that he was back on the island. And then, without a word, Holly slipped her hand in his. Then again, this wasn't so bad.

She leaned over and softly said, "Relax. You might even find you like the holiday."

"Maybe you're right." He had his doubts, but he didn't want to give her any reason to back out of their arrangement. He only had until the first of the year to convince her that they were better off together than apart.

"We turned the wrong way. This is the opposite direction of my apartment." Obvious concern laced Holly's words. "Hey!" She waved, trying to gain the driver's attention. "We need to turn around."

"No, we don't," Finn said calmly. "It's okay, Ron. I've got this."

"You've got what?" She frowned at him.

"I've instructed Ron to drive us back to my penthouse—"

"What? No. I need to go home."

"Not yet. You heard the doctor. You have a high-risk pregnancy and your blood pressure is elevated—"

"Only slightly."

"She said not to overdo it. And from what you've told me, your apartment is a fifth-floor walk-up with no elevator."

"It… It's not that much. I'm used to it."

He wasn't going to change his mind about this arrangement. It was what was best for her and the babies. "And then there's the fact that your mother is out of town. There's no one around if you have any complications."

"I won't have any." Her hand moved to rest protectively over her slightly rounded midsection. "Nothing is going to happen."

"I sincerely hope you're right, but is it worth the risk? If you're wrong—"

"I won't be. But…your idea might not be so bad. As long as you understand that it's only temporary. Until my next appointment."

Which was at the beginning of the new year—not far off. "We'll see what the doctor says then. Now will you relax?"

"As long as you understand that this arrangement doesn't change anything between us—I'm still not accepting your proposal."

He wanted to tell her that she was wrong, but he couldn't. Maybe he was asking too much of her—of himself. He couldn't promise her forever.

An ache started deep in his chest.

What if he made her unhappy?

Maybe he was being selfish instead of doing what was best for Holly.

CHAPTER EIGHTEEN

IT DIDN'T FEEL like Christmas.

Holly strolled into the living room of Finn's penthouse. There was absolutely nothing that resembled Christmas anywhere. She knew he avoided the holiday because of the bad memories it held for him, but she wondered if it would be possible to create some new holiday memories.

She'd been here for two days and, so far, Finn had bent over backward to make her at home. He'd set her up in his study to monitor the final stages of Project Santa. And so far they'd only encountered minor glitches. It was nothing that couldn't be overcome with a bit of ingenuity.

That morning when she'd offered to go into the office, Finn had waved her off, telling her to stay here. Meanwhile, he'd gone to the office to pick up some papers. He'd said he'd be back in a couple of hours, but that was before lunch. And now it was after quitting time and he still wasn't back.

Perhaps this was the best opportunity for her to take care of something that had been weighing on her mind. She retraced her steps to the study where she'd left her phone. She had Finn's number on it because he refused to leave until he had entered it in her phone with orders for her to call if she needed anything at all.

Certain in her plan, she selected his number and listened to the phone ring. Once. That's all it rang before Finn answered. "Holly, what's the matter?"

"Does something have to be the matter?"

"No. I just… Oh, never mind, what did you need?"

"I wanted you to know that I'm going out. There's something I need to take care of."

"I'm almost home. Can I pick something up for you?"

"It's more like I have to drop off something."

"Tonight?" His voice sounded off.

"Yes, tonight."

"I just heard the weather report and they're calling for snow. A lot of it."

Holly glanced toward the window. "It's not snowing yet. I won't be gone long. I'll most likely be home before it starts."

"Holly, put it off—"

"No. I need to do this." She'd been thinking about it all day. Once the visit with her family was over, she could relax. It'd definitely help lower her blood pressure.

Finn expelled a heavy sigh. "If you aren't going to change your mind, at least let me drive you."

He had no idea what this trip entailed. To say her family dynamics were complicated was an understatement. It was best Finn stay home. "Thanks. But I'm sure you have other things to do—"

"Nothing as important as you."

The breath caught in her throat. Had he really just said that? Was she truly important to him? And then she realized he probably meant because she was carrying his babies. Because she'd asked him straight up if he loved her and he hadn't been able to say the words.

"Holly? Are you still there?"

"Um, yes."

"Good. I'm just pulling into the garage now. I'll be up in a minute. Just be ready to go."

She disconnected the call and moved to her spacious bedroom to retrieve the Christmas packages and her coat. Her stomach churned. Once this was done, she could relax. In and out quickly.

She'd just carried the packages to the foyer when Finn let himself in the door. She glanced up at him. "You know I can take a cab."

"I told you if you're going out tonight, I'm going with you."

"You don't even know where I'm going."

"Good point. What's our destination?"

"My father's house. I want to give my sisters the Christmas presents I bought while we were in the Caribbean."

He scooped up the packages before opening the door for her. "So we've progressed to the point where I get to meet the family." Finn sent her a teasing smile. "I don't know. Do you think I'll pass the father inspection?"

She stopped at the elevator and pressed the button before turning back to him. "I don't think you have a thing to worry about."

His smile broadened. "That's nice to know."

"Don't get any ideas. In fact, you can wait in the car. I won't be long."

"Are you sure you want to take the presents now? I mean Christmas isn't until the weekend after next."

"I don't spend Christmas with them. I usually spend it with my mother. But after talking with my mother and aunt, I decided to give them something extra special for Christmas—a cruise." It would definitely put a dent in her savings, but it was worth it. This was her mother's dream vacation.

"That was very generous of you."

Holly's voice lowered. "They deserve it."

"And what about you?" When she sent him a puzzled look, he added, "You deserve a special Christmas, too. What would you like Santa to bring you?"

"I… I don't know. I hadn't thought about it."

The elevator door slid open. Finn waited until Holly stepped inside before he followed. "You know without your mother around, perhaps you could spend the time with your father."

She shook her head. "I don't think that would be a good idea."

Finn had no idea about her family. Thankfully she'd thought to tell him to stay in the car. She didn't want to make an awkward situation even more so.

Something was amiss, but what?

Was she really that uncomfortable with him meeting her family? Or was it something else? Finn glanced over at Holly just before he pulled out from a stop sign. The wipers swished back and forth, knocking off the gently falling snow.

The sky was dark now and all Finn wanted to do was turn around. He wasn't worried about himself. He never let the weather stop him from being wherever he was needed. But it was different now that he had Holly next to him and those precious babies. He worried about the roads becoming slick.

"We're almost there." Holly's voice drew him from his thoughts.

It was the first thing she'd said in blocks. In fact, she hadn't volunteered any details about her family. Why was that?

As he proceeded through the next intersection, Holly pointed to a modest two-story white house with a well-kept yard that was now coated with snow. "There it is."

He pulled over to the curb and turned off his wipers. "You've been awfully quiet. Is everything all right?"

"Sure. Why wouldn't it be?"

"You haven't said a word the whole way here unless it was to give me directions."

"Oh. Sorry. I must be tired."

"Sounds like a good reason to head back to the penthouse and deal with this another day."

"No." She released the seat belt. "We're here now. And I want to get this over with."

"Okay. It's up to you."

When he released his seat belt and opened the door, she asked, "What are you doing?"

"Getting the packages from the trunk."

She really didn't want him to meet her family. Why was she so worried? He didn't think he made that bad of a first impression. In fact, when he tried he could be pretty charming. And if they were going to be a family, which they were because of the babies, he needed to meet her father. He was certain he could make a good impression and alleviate Holly's worries.

With the packages in hand, he closed the trunk and started up the walk. Every step was muffled by the thin layer of snow.

"Where do you think you're going?" Holly remained next to the car.

He turned back and noticed the way the big flakes coated the top of her head like a halo. "I presume we're taking the presents to the door and not leaving them in the front yard."

"There's no *we* about it."

"Listen, Holly, you've got to trust me. This will all work out."

"You're right. It will. You're going to wait in the car." Her tone brooked no room for a rebuttal.

Just then there was a noise behind him. "Who's there?" called out a male voice. "Holly, is that you?"

She glared at Finn before her face morphed into a smile. "Yes, Dad. It's me."

"Well, are you coming in?"

Obediently she started up the walk. When she got to Finn's side, she leaned closer and whispered, "Just let me do the talking."

Boy, she was really worried about having him around her family. "Trust me."

He wasn't sure if she'd heard his softly spoken words as

she continued up the walk. He followed behind her, wondering what to expect.

They stopped on the stoop. Her father was still blocking the doorway. The man's hair was dark with silver in the temples. He wore dark jeans and a sweatshirt with the Jets logo across the front. Finn made a mental note of it. If all else failed, maybe he could engage the man in football talk—even though he was more of a hockey fan.

"Who's at the door?" a female voice called out.

"It's Holly and some guy."

"Well, invite them in." And then a slender woman with long, bleached-blond hair appeared next to Holly's father. The woman elbowed her husband aside. "Don't mind him. Come in out of the cold."

Once they were all standing just inside the door, Finn could feel the stress coming off Holly in waves. What was up with that? Was she embarrassed of him? That would be a first. Most women liked to show him off to their friends. As for meeting a date's family, he avoided that at all costs. But Holly was different.

"Here, let me take your coats." Holly's stepmother didn't smile as she held out her hand. She kept giving Finn a look as though she should know him but couldn't quite place his face.

"That's okay." Holly didn't make any move to get comfortable. "We can't stay. I… I brought some gifts for the girls."

"Suzie! Kristi! Holly's here with gifts."

"I hope they like them. I saw them while I was out of town and thought of them."

"I'm sure they will." But there was no conviction in the woman's voice. "You can afford to go on vacation?"

Holly's face paled. "It was a business trip."

"Oh."

Her father retreated into the living room, which was off

to the right of the doorway. A staircase stood in front of them with a hallway trailing along the left side of it. And to the far left was a formal dining room. The house wasn't big, but it held a look of perfection—as though everything was in its place. There was nothing warm and welcoming about the house.

Finn wanted to say something to break up the awkward silence, but he wasn't sure what to say. Was it always this strained? If so, he understood why Holly wouldn't want to spend much time here.

"Who's your friend?" Her stepmother's gaze settled fully on him.

"Oh. This is Finn. He's my—"

"Boyfriend. It's nice to meet you." He held out his hand to the woman.

"I'm Helen." She flashed him a big, toothy smile as she accepted his handshake. "I feel like I should know you. Have we met before?"

"No."

"Are you sure?" She still held on to his hand.

He gently extracted his hand while returning her smile. "I'm certain of it. I wouldn't have forgotten meeting someone as lovely as you."

Her painted cheeks puffed up. "Well, I'm glad we've had a chance to meet. Isn't that right, Fred?" And then at last noticing that her husband had settled in the living room with a newspaper, she raised her voice. "Fred, you're ignoring our guests."

The man glanced over the top of his reading glasses. "You seem to be doing fine on your own."

"Don't I always?" the woman muttered under her breath. "Lately that man is hardly home. All he does is work." She moved to the bottom of the steps and craned her chin upward. "Suzie! Kristi! Get down here now!"

Doors slammed almost simultaneously. There was a rush

of footsteps as they crossed the landing and then stomped down the stairs.

"What do you want? I'm busy doing my nails." A teenage girl with hair similar to her mother's frowned.

"And I'm on the phone." The other teenager had dark hair with pink highlights.

"I know you're both busy, but I thought you'd want to know that your sister is here."

Both girls glanced toward the door. But they were staring—at him.

Both girls' eyes grew round. "Hey, you're Finn Lockwood." They continued down the steps and approached him. "What are you doing here?"

His stomach churned as they both batted their eyes at him and flashed him smiles.

"He's your sister's boyfriend."

Surprise lit up both sets of eyes. "You're dating her?"

He nodded. "I am. Your sister is amazing."

"I brought you some gifts." Holly stepped next to Finn. "I found them when I was in the Caribbean and I thought you would like them."

Each girl accepted a brightly wrapped package.

"What do you say?" prompted their mother.

"Thank you," they muttered to Holly.

"I'm Suzie," said the blonde.

"And I'm Kristi."

Helen stepped between her daughters. "Why don't you come in the living room and we can talk?"

"We really can't stay." Holly glanced at him with uncertainty in her eyes.

He smiled at her. "Holly's right. We have other obligations tonight, but she was anxious for me to meet you all."

"How did she bag you?" Suzie's brows drew together. "You're a billionaire and she's nothing."

Ouch! Finn's gaze went to the stepmother, but Helen

glanced away as though she hadn't heard a word. That was impossible because Suzie's voice was loud and quite clear.

His gaze settled back on Suzie. "Holly is amazing. She is quite talented. And she spearheaded the Project Santa initiative."

"The what?"

"It's nothing," Holly intervened. "We really should go."

Finn took Holly's hand in his. "We have a couple of minutes and they haven't opened their gifts yet."

Both girls glanced down as though they'd forgotten about the Christmas presents. They each pulled off the ribbons first and then tore through the wrapping paper. They lifted the lids and rooted through the bikinis and cover up as well as sunglasses and a small purse.

Kristi glanced up. "Does this mean you got us tickets to the Caribbean? My friends are going to be so jealous. I'll have to go to the tanning salon first. Otherwise I'll look like a snowman in a bikini."

Suzie's face lit up. "This will be great. I can't wait to get out of school."

"Oh, girls, we'll have to make sure you have everything you need. I'll need to go to the tanning salon, too."

"You?" The girls both turned to their mother.

"This is our gift, not yours," Suzie said bluntly. "You aren't invited."

"But—"

"Um, there is no trip," Holly said.

"No trip?" All heads turned to Holly. "You mean all you got us was some bikinis that we can't even use because if you hadn't noticed, it's snowing outside—"

"Suzie, that's enough. I'm sure your sister has something else in mind." Her stepmother sent her an expectant look.

Wow! This family was unbelievable. If Finn had his choice between having no family and this family, he'd be much happier on his own. He glanced around to find out why Holly's father hadn't interceded on his daughter's behalf, but the man couldn't be bothered to stop reading his paper long enough.

Finn inwardly seethed. As much as he'd like to let loose on these people and tell them exactly what he thought of them and their lack of manners, he had to think of Holly. For whatever reason, they meant enough to her to buy them gifts and come here to put up with their rudeness. Therefore, he had to respect her feelings because it certainly appeared that no one else would.

"There is one other thing." Finn looked at Holly, willing her to trust him with his eyes as he gave her hand a couple of quick squeezes. "Do you want me to tell them?"

"Um…uh, sure."

"You know how Holly is, never wanting to brag. But she used her connections and secured tickets to the Mistletoe Ball for the whole family."

For once, all three females were left speechless. Good. That was what he wanted.

"You did that? But how?" Her stepmother's eyes reflected her utter surprise. "Those tickets cost a fortune and I heard they sold out back in October."

Holly's face drained of color. "Well, the truth is—"

"She has an inside source that she promised not to reveal to anyone," Finn said. "They'll be waiting for the four of you at the door of the museum."

The girls squealed with delight as Helen yelled in to her husband to tell him about the tickets to the ball. If a man could look utterly unimpressed, it was Holly's father. And through it all, Finn noticed that not one person thanked Holly. It was though they felt entitled to the tickets. A groan of frustration grew down deep in his throat. A glance at Holly's pale face had him swallowing down his outrage and disgust.

He made a point of checking his Rolex. "And now, we really must be going."

As they let themselves out the front door, the girls were talking over top of each other about dresses, shoes, haircuts and manicures. And he had never been so happy to leave anywhere in his entire life. Once outside, Finn felt as though he could breathe. He was no longer being smothered with fake pleasantries and outright nastiness.

CHAPTER NINETEEN

BIG FLUFFY SNOWFLAKES fell around them, adding a gentle softness to the world and smoothing out the rough edges. Finn continued to hold Holly's hand, enjoying the connection. When they reached the car, he used his free hand to open the door.

She paused.

"Holly?"

When she looked up at him, tears shimmered in her eyes. The words lodged in his throat. There was nothing in this world that he could say to lessen the pain for her.

Instead of speaking, he leaned forward and pressed his lips to hers. With the car door ajar between them, he couldn't pull her close like he wanted. Instead he had to be content with this simple but heartfelt gesture.

With great regret he pulled back. "You better get in. The snow is picking up."

She nodded and then did as he said.

Once they were on the now snow-covered road, Finn guided the car slowly along the streets. He should have been more insistent about putting off this visit, not that Holly would have listened to him. When she set her mind on something, there was no stopping her. Although after meeting her family, he could understand why she'd want to get that visit out of the way.

As the snow fell, covering up the markings on the street, his body tensed. This must have been how it'd been the night his parents died. The thought sent a chill through his body.

"Are you cold?" Holly asked.

"What?"

"I just saw you shiver. I'll turn up the fan. Hopefully the heat will kick in soon." After she adjusted the temperature controls, she leaned back in her seat. "What were you think-ing by offering up those tickets to the ball? I don't have any connections."

"But I do. So don't worry." He didn't want to carry on a conversation now.

"You...you shouldn't have done it. It's too much."

"Sure, I should have." Not taking his eyes off the road, he reached out to her. His hand landed on her thigh and he squeezed. "I wanted to do it for you. I know how much your family means to you."

"They shouldn't, though. I know they don't treat me...like family. I just wish—oh, I don't know what I wish."

"It's done now so stop worrying." He returned his hand to the steering wheel.

"That's easy for you to say. You're not related to them."

"But they are related to you and the babies. Therefore, they are now part of my life." He could feel her eyeing him up. Had that been too strong? He didn't think so. Even if he never won over her heart, they would all still be one mixed-up sort of family.

"You do know what this means, don't you?"

His fingers tightened on the steering wheel, not liking the sound of her voice. "What?"

"That you and I must go to the ball now. And it's a well-known fact that you make a point of never attending the ball."

"For you, I'll make an exception." The snow came down heavier, making his every muscle tense. "Don't worry. It'll all work out."

"I'll pay you back."

Just then the tires started to slide. His heart lurched. *No! No! No!*

Holly reached out, placing a hand on his thigh. Her fin-gers tightened, but she didn't say a word.

When the tires caught on the asphalt, Finn expelled a pent-up breath. This was his fault. He promised to take care of his family and protect them like he hadn't been able to do with his parents and brother. And already he was failing.

Finn swallowed hard. "If you want to pay me back, the next time I tell you that we should stay in because of the weather, just listen to me."

She didn't say anything for a moment. And then ever so softly, she said, "I'm sorry. I didn't think it'd get this bad."

His fingers tightened on the steering wheel as he lowered his speed even more, wishing that they were closer to his building.

Just a little farther. Everything will be all right. It has to be.

His gut twisted into a knot. It was going to take him a long time to unwind after this. The snow kept falling, making visibility minimal at best. The wipers cleared the windshield in time for more snow to cover it.

His thoughts turned back to Holly. The truth was that no matter how much he'd fought it in the beginning, he'd fallen for Holly, hook, line and sinker. He couldn't bear to lose her or the babies. From now on, when they went out, he'd plan ahead. He'd be cautious. He'd do anything it took to keep them safe.

From here on out, they were a team. He had Holly's back. And he already knew that she had his—the success of Project Santa was evidence of it. Now he just had to concentrate on the roadway and make sure they didn't end up skidding into a ditch or worse.

What an utter disaster.

Back at the penthouse, Holly didn't know what to say to Finn. He'd been so quiet in the car. He must be upset that she let him walk into such a strained situation and then for him to feel obligated to come up with those tickets to the ball. They cost a small fortune. She didn't know how she'd ever repay him.

Now she was having second thoughts about telling Finn that they had to go to the ball. She didn't know how she'd explain it to her family, but she'd come up with a reason for their absence. Besides, it wasn't like she even had a dress, and the ball was just days away.

When she stepped into the living room, she found Finn had on the Rangers and Penguins hockey game. That was good. After the cleanup on the island, the work at the office and then meeting her family, he deserved some downtime.

She sat down on the couch near him. "I hope you don't mind that I ordered pizza for dinner."

"That's fine." His voice was soft as though he was lost in thought.

"Tomorrow I'll work on getting some food in the fridge."

He didn't say anything.

She glanced up at the large-screen television. She had to be honest, she didn't know anything about hockey or for that matter any other sport, but she might need to if these babies were anything like their father.

"Who's winning?"

He didn't say anything.

What was wrong with him? Was he mad at her? She hoped not. Maybe he was just absorbed by the game. "Who's winning?"

"What?"

"The score. What is it?"

"I don't know."

He didn't know? Wasn't he watching the game? But as she glanced at him, she noticed he was staring out the window at the snowy night. Okay, something was wrong and she couldn't just let it fester. If he had changed his mind about her staying here, she wanted to know up front. She realized she came with a lot of baggage and if he wanted out, she couldn't blame him.

She placed a hand on his arm. "Finn, talk to me."

He glanced at her. "What do you want to talk about?"

"Whatever's bothering you?"

"Nothing's bothering me." He glanced away.

"You might have been able to tell me that a while back, but now that I know you, I don't believe you. Something has been bothering you since we left my father's. It's my family, isn't it?"

"What? No. Of course not."

"Listen, I know those tickets are going to cost a fortune. I will pay you back."

"No, you won't. They are my gift. And so is your dress and whatever else you need for the ball."

"But I couldn't accept all of that. It… It's too much."

"The ball was my idea, not yours, so no arguments. Tomorrow we'll go to this boutique I know of that should have something for you to wear. If not, we'll keep looking."

"I don't know what to say."

"Good. Don't say anything. I just want you to enjoy yourself."

"But how am I supposed to after tonight? I'm really sorry about my family. It's complicated with them. I was less than cordial to my stepmother when she married my father. I blamed her for breaking up my parents' marriage since he had an ongoing affair with her for a couple of years before he left my mother."

Finn's gaze met hers. "And your mother didn't know?"

Holly shrugged. "She says she didn't, but I don't know how she couldn't know. He was gone all the time. But maybe it was a case of *she didn't want to know so she didn't look*."

"Sometimes we protect ourselves by only seeing as much as we can handle."

"Maybe you're right. But I think my mother's happy now. I just want to keep her that way, because she did her best to be there for me and now it's my turn to be there for her."

"And you will be. I see how you stick by those you love."

"You mean how I still go to my father's house even though I'll never be one of them?"

"I didn't mean that."

"It's okay. I realize this, but as much as they can grate on my nerves, I also know that for better or worse, they are my family. I just insist on taking them in small doses. And I'm so sorry I let you walk into that—I should have made it clearer to you—"

"It's okay, Holly. You didn't do anything wrong."

"But you didn't talk on the way home."

"That had nothing to do with your family and everything to do with me and my poor judgment. I'm forever putting those I care about at risk."

Wait. Where did that come from? "I don't understand. You didn't put me at risk."

"Yes, I did. And it can't happen again. We shouldn't have been out on the roads tonight. We could have…"

"Could have what? Talk to me."

He sighed. "Maybe if I tell you, you'll understand why I don't deserve to be happy."

"Of course you do." She took his hand and pressed it to her slightly rounded abdomen. "And these babies are proof of it."

"You might change your mind after I tell you this."

"I highly doubt it, but I'm listening."

"It had been a snowy February night a year after my brother died. I'd been invited to my best friend's birthday party, but I wasn't going. I was jealous of my friend because my Christmas had come and gone without lights and a tree. I'd been given a couple of gift cards, more as an afterthought."

Holly settled closer to him. She rested her head on his shoulder as she slipped her hand in his. She didn't know where he was going with this story, but wherever it led, she'd be there with him.

"My birthday had been in January—my thirteenth birthday—I was so excited to be a teenager. You know how kids are, always in a rush to grow up. But my parents hadn't done anything for it. There was no surprise party—no friends invited over—just a store-bought cake that didn't even have my name on it. I was given one birthday gift. There were apologies and promises to make it up to me."

Her heart ached for him. She moved her other hand over and rested it on his arm.

"When the phone rang to find out why I wasn't at my friend's party, my mother insisted I go and take a gift. Our parents were close friends, so when I again refused to go, my mother took back the one birthday gift that I'd received but refused to open. She insisted on delivering it to the party, but the snow was mounting outside and she was afraid to drive. My father reluctantly agreed to drive, but not before calling me a selfish brat and ordering me to my room."

Finn inhaled a ragged breath as he squeezed her hand. She couldn't imagine how much he'd lived through as a child. The death of his brother had spun the whole family out of control. No wonder he was such a hands-on leader. He knew the devastating consequences of losing control.

Finn's voice grew softer. "They only had a few blocks to drive, but the roads were icy. They had to cross a major roadway. My father had been going too fast. When he slowed down for the red light, he hit a patch of ice and slid into the intersection…into the path of two oncoming vehicles."

"Oh, Finn. Is that what happened tonight? You were reliving your parents' accident?"

He nodded. "Don't you see? If I had gone to that party, I would have been there before the snow. My parents would have never been out on the road. And tonight if I had paid attention to the forecast, I would have known about the storm rolling in."

"No matter how much you want to, you can't control the future. You had no idea then or now about what was going to happen. You can't hold yourself responsible."

"But you and those babies are my responsibility. If anything had happened to you, I wouldn't have known what to do with myself."

"You'd lean on your friends."

He shook his head. "I don't have friends. I have associates at best."

"Maybe if you let down your guard, you'd find out those people really do like you for you and not for what you can do for them." Her mind started to weave a plan to show Finn that he didn't need to be all alone in this world.

"I don't know. I've kept to myself so long. I wouldn't know how to change—how to let people in."

"I bet it's easier than you're thinking. Look how quickly we became friends."

"Is that what we are?" His gaze delved deep into her as though he could see straight through to the secrets lurking within her heart. "Are we just friends?"

Her heart *thump-thumped*. They were so much more than friends, but her voice failed her. Maybe words weren't necessary. In this moment actions would speak so much louder.

Need thrummed in her veins. She needed to let go of her insecurities. She needed to feel connected to him—to feel the love and happiness he brought to her life. She needed all of Finn with a force that almost scared her.

He filled in those cracks and crevices in her heart, making it whole. And not even her father's indifference tonight, her stepmother's coldness or her stepsisters' rudeness could touch her now. In this moment the only person that mattered was the man holding her close.

So while the snow fell outside, Holly melted into Finn's arms. She couldn't think of any other place she'd rather be and no one else she'd rather be with on this cold, blustery night.

CHAPTER TWENTY

THIS WAS IT.

Holly stared at her reflection in the mirror. The blue sparkly gown clung to her figure—showing the beginning of her baby bump. She frowned. What had she been thinking? Perhaps she should have selected something loose that hid her figure. But Finn had insisted this dress was his favorite. She turned this way and that way in front of the mirror. And truth be told, she did like it—a lot.

She took a calming breath. She was nervous about her first public outing on the arm of New York's most eligible bachelor. A smile pulled at her lips as she thought of Finn. He'd been so kind and generous supplying her family with tickets to the ball, and now she had a surprise for him.

It'd taken a bit of secrecy and a lot of help, but she'd pulled together an evening that Finn would not soon forget. To put the plan into action, she'd needed to get rid of him for just a bit. Unable to come up with a better excuse, she'd pleaded that her prenatal vitamin prescription needed refilling. To her surprise he'd jumped at the opportunity to go to the store. She might have worried about his eagerness to leave if her mind wasn't already on the details of her surprise. She liked to think of it as Project Finn.

She smoothed a hand over her up-do hairstyle. It was secured by an army of hairpins. Nothing could move it now. She then swiped a wand of pink gloss over her lips. She felt like she was forgetting something, but she couldn't figure out what it might be.

The doorbell rang. It was time for the evening's festivities to begin. She rushed to the door and flung it open to find Clara standing there on the arm of her new husband. They were each holding a large shopping bag.

"Hi." Holly's gaze moved to Clara's husband. "I'm Holly. It's so nice to meet you."

"I'm Steve." He shook her hand. "Clara had a lot to say about you and Finn—all good. I swear."

Holly couldn't blame Clara. From the outside, she and Finn appeared to be an overnight romance. No one knew that it started a few months ago.

Then remembering her manners, she moved aside. "Please come inside. I sent Finn out on an errand. Hopefully he won't be back for a little bit. Is everything going according to plan?"

Clara nodded. "It is. Are you sure about this?"

"Yes." Her response sounded more certain than she felt at the moment. "This is my Christmas present to Finn."

"I didn't know he did Christmas presents."

"He doesn't, but that's all going to change now."

"Isn't this place amazing?" Clara glanced all around. "I'm always in awe of it every time I stop by with some papers for him. And as expected, there's not a single Christmas decoration in sight." Clara sent Holly a hesitant look. "Do you really think this is going to work?"

"As long as you have the ornaments in those bags, we're only missing the tree."

"Don't worry. I called on my way over and the tree is on its way."

"Oh, good. Thank you so much. I couldn't have done this without you. But no worries. If it doesn't go the way I planned, you're safe. I'll take full responsibility."

Holly thought of mentioning the baby news. She was getting anxious to tell people, but she didn't know how Finn would feel about her telling his PA without him. So she remained quiet—for now.

After pointing out where she thought a Christmas tree

would look best, Holly asked, "Where's everyone else? I was hoping they'd be here before he gets back."

As if on cue, the doorbell rang again.

"That must be them. I'll get it." Clara rushed over and swung open the door. "I was starting to wonder what happened to you guys."

A string of people came through the door carrying a Christmas tree and packages. Some people Holly recognized from the office and others were new to her. They were all invited to Finn's penthouse before attending the Mistletoe Ball. In all, there was close to a dozen people in the penthouse. Clara made sure to introduce Holly to all of them. Everyone was smiling and talking as they set to work decking Finn's halls with strands of twinkle light, garland and mistletoe.

Holly couldn't help but wonder what Finn would make of this impromptu Christmas party.

As though Clara could read her mind, she leaned in close. "Don't worry. He'll like this. Thanks to you, he's a changed man."

Holly wasn't so sure, but she hoped Clara was right. Instead of worrying, she joined the others as they trimmed the tree.

How long does it take to fill a prescription?

Finn rocked back on his heels, tired of standing in one spot. He checked his watch for the tenth time in ten minutes. There was plenty of time before they had to leave for the ball. Not that he wanted to go, but once he'd invited Holly's family there was no backing out.

He made a point of never going to the ball. Publicly, he distanced himself as much as he could from the event. He liked to think of himself as the man behind the magic curtain. He never felt worthy to take any of the credit for the prestigious event. He carried so much guilt around with him—always feeling like a poor replacement for his family.

But Holly was changing his outlook on life. Maybe she had a point—maybe punishing himself wasn't helping anyone.

He strolled through the aisles of the pharmacy. When he got to the baby aisle, he stopped. He gazed at the shelves crowded with formula, toys and diapers. All of this was needed for a baby? Oh, boy! He had no idea what most of the gizmos even did.

Then the image of the twins filled his mind. His fingers traced over a pacifier. He finally acknowledged to himself that he had to let go of the ghosts that haunted him if he had any hopes of embracing the future. Because deep down he wanted Holly and those babies more than anything in the world.

In no time, he was headed back to the penthouse with two pacifiers tucked in his inner jacket pocket and roses in his hand. He knew what he needed to do now. He needed to tell Holly how much he loved her and their babies—how he couldn't live without them.

But when he swung open the penthouse door, he came to a complete standstill. There were people everywhere. In front of the window now stood a Christmas tree. It was like he'd stepped into Santa's hideaway at the North Pole.

Where had all of these people come from? He studied their faces. Most were his coworkers. The unfamiliar faces he assumed were significant others. But where was Holly?

He closed the door and stepped farther into the room. People turned and smiled. Men shook his hand and women told him what a lovely home he had. He welcomed them and gave the appropriate responses all the while wondering what in the world they were doing there.

And then a hand touched his shoulder. He turned, finding Clara standing there, smiling at him. If this was her idea, they were going to have a long talk—a very long talk.

"Oh, I know who those are for. Nice touch." Clara sent him a smile of approval.

"What?"

She pointed to his hand.

Glancing down at the bouquet of red roses he'd picked up on his way home, he decided to give them to Holly later—when it was just the two of them. He moved off to the side and laid them on a shelf.

Finding Clara still close at hand, he turned back to her. "Looks like I arrived in time for the party."

"What do you think? Holly went all out planning this get-together."

Holly? She did this? "But why? I don't understand."

Clara shrugged. "Holly didn't tell me what prompted this little party. Maybe she just thought it would be a nice gesture before the ball. All I know is that she asked me to pull together all of your close friends."

Close friends? He turned to his PA and arched a brow. "And now you take directions from Holly?"

"Seemed like the right thing to do. After all, I'm all for helping the course of true love."

He turned away, afraid Clara would read too much in his eyes. True love? Were his feelings that obvious?

"Just be good to her. She's a special person." And with that, Clara went to mingle with the others.

His close friends? He glanced around the room. Yes, he knew many of these people. They'd been the ones to help him when he'd been old enough to step into his father's role as CEO. He'd had lunch or dinner with all of them at one point or another. He'd even discussed sports and family with them. He'd never thought it was any more than them being polite and doing what was expected, but maybe he hadn't been willing to admit that those connections had meant so much more.

Finn recalled the other night when he'd been snuggled with Holly on the couch. They'd been discussing friends and he'd said he didn't have any. Was this Holly's way of showing him that he wasn't alone in this world? That if he let down his guard, this could be his?

"Finn, there you are." Holly rushed up to him. "I have some explaining to do."

"I think I understand."

Her beautiful eyes widened. "You do?"

He nodded before he leaned down. With his mouth near hers, he whispered, "Thank you."

And then with all of his—their—friends around, he kissed her. And it wasn't just a peck. No, this was a passionate kiss and he didn't care who witnessed it. He was in love.

CHAPTER TWENTY-ONE

HOLLY COULDN'T STOP SMILING.

A 1950s big-band tune echoed through the enormous lobby of the Metropolitan Museum. It was Holly's first visit and she was awed by the amazing architecture, not to mention the famous faces in attendance, from professional athletes to movie stars. It was a Who's Who of New York.

It also didn't hurt that she was in the arms of the most handsome man. Holly lifted her chin in order to look up at Finn. This evening was the beginning of big things to come—she was certain of it.

Finn's gaze caught hers. "Are you having fun?"

"The time of my life. But you shouldn't be spending all of your time with me. There are a lot of people who want to speak with you, including the paparazzi out in front of the museum."

"The reporters always have questions."

"Did you even listen to any of them?"

"No. I don't want anyone or anything to ruin this evening."

"You don't understand. It's good news. In fact, it's great news. Project Santa was such a success that it garnered national attention. The website is getting hit after hit and tons of heartfelt thank-yous from project coordinators, outreach workers and parents. There have even been phone calls from other companies wanting to participate next year. Just think of all the children and families that could be helped."

Finn smiled. "And it's all thanks to you."

"Me?" She shook her head. "It was your idea."

"But it was your ingenuity that saved the project. You took a project that started as a corporate endeavor and put it in the hands of the employees and the community. To me, that's the true meaning of Christmas—people helping people."

His words touched her deeply. "Thank you. I really connected with the project and the people behind the scenes."

"And that's why I think you should take it over permanently. Just let me know what you need."

Holly stopped dancing. "Seriously?"

"I've never been more serious."

This was the most fulfilling job she'd ever had. She didn't have to think it over. She knew this was her calling. Not caring that they were in the middle of the dance floor, she lifted on her toes and kissed him.

When they made it to the edge of the dance floor, Finn was drawn away from her by a group of men needing his opinion on something. Holly smiled, enjoying watching Finn animated and outgoing.

Out of excuses, Holly made her way to her family. It was time she said hello. She made small talk with her stepmother and sisters, but her father was nowhere to be seen. As usual, they quickly ran out of things to say to each other and Holly made her departure.

On the other side of the dance floor, Holly spotted her father dancing too close with a young lady. He was chatting her up while the young woman smiled broadly. Then her father leaned closer, whispering in the woman's ear. The woman blushed.

The whole scene sickened Holly—reminding her of all the reasons she'd sworn off men. They just couldn't be trusted and it apparently didn't get better with age.

Her stepmother was in for a painful reality check when she found out that she'd been traded in for a younger model just like her father had done to Holly's mother. The thought didn't make Holly happy. It made her very sad because she knew all too well the pain her half-sisters were about to experience.

Deciding she wasn't in any frame of mind to make friendly chitchat, she veered toward a quiet corner. She needed to gather herself. And then a beautiful woman stepped in her path. Holly didn't recognize her, but apparently the woman knew her.

"Hi, Holly. I've been meaning to get a moment to speak with you." The polished woman in a red sparkly dress held out a manicured hand.

"Hi." Holly shook her hand, all the while experiencing a strange sensation that she should know this woman.

Her confusion must have registered on her face because the woman said, "I'm sorry. I should have introduced myself. I'm Meryl."

Surely she couldn't be Finn's ex, could she? But there was no way Holly was going to ask that question. If she was wrong, it would be humiliating. And if she was right, well, awkwardness would ensue.

"If you're wondering, yes, I am that Meryl. But don't worry, Finn and I were over ages ago. I saw you earlier, dancing with him. I've never seen him look so happy. I'm guessing you're the one to do that for him. He's a very lucky man."

At last, the shock subsided and Holly found her voice. "It's really nice to meet you. Finn has nothing but good things to say about you."

Meryl's eyes lit up. "That's good to know. I think he's pretty great, too."

Really? Finn had given her the impression that hard feelings lingered. Her gaze scanned the crowd for the man they had in common, but she didn't see him anywhere.

"Ah, I see I caught you by surprise." The woman's voice was gentle and friendly. "You thought there would be lots of hard feelings, but there aren't. I assure you. Finn is a very generous and kind man. He just doesn't give himself enough credit."

"I agree with you."

Holly wanted desperately to dislike this woman, but she couldn't. Meryl seemed so genuine—so down to earth. There was a kindness that reflected in her eyes. Why exactly had Finn let her get away?

"And the fact that you were able to get him to attend his very own ball is a big credit to you."

"His ball?"

The woman's eyes widened in surprise. "I'm sorry. I said too much."

"No, you didn't." Holly needed to know what was going on. "Why did you call this Finn's ball? As far as I know, he's never even attended before this year."

"I thought he would have told you, especially since he just told me that he intends to marry you."

"He told you that?"

The woman nodded as her brows scrunched together. "Anyway, I do the leg work for the ball, but he's the drive behind it. It's not made public but the ball is done in memory of Finn's mother and brother. He says that he remains in the background underwriting all of the associated expenses because he's made a number of unpopular business deals as far as the press is concerned, but I think it's something else."

The thought that this woman had insights into Finn that Holly lacked bothered her. "What do you think his reasons are?"

"I think the ball reminds him of his family and for whatever reason, he carries a truckload of guilt that he survived and they didn't."

And that was where Holly was able to fill in the missing pieces, but she kept what Finn had told her about his past to herself. She knew all about his survivor's guilt. And now she realized how much it'd cost him to come here tonight.

But what other secrets was he keeping from me? Tears stung the backs of her eyes. *Stupid hormones.* "There appears to be a lot I have to learn about Finn."

"I'm not surprised he didn't mention it. Finn doesn't open up easily."

Just to those that are closest to him. Holly finished Meryl's statement. After all of their talk about being open and honest with each other, he let her come here not knowing the facts. He'd lied to her by omission. Now she wondered what else he was keeping from her.

"I... I should be going." Holly was anxious to be alone with her thoughts.

"Well, there I go putting my foot in my mouth. Sorry about that. Sometimes when I'm nervous I talk too much."

"It's okay. I've really enjoyed talking with you."

Meryl's eyes lit up as a smile returned to her face. "I'm really glad we met. I think we might just end up friends, of course if you're willing."

"I'd like that."

But as they parted company, Holly didn't think their friendship would ever have a chance to flourish. She doubted they'd ever run into each other again.

She turned to come face-to-face with her father. He was the very last person she wanted to speak to that evening. "Excuse me."

Her father stepped in front of her. "Not so fast. I did a little research into that boyfriend of yours. And I think I should get to know him better."

Not a chance. Her father caused enough destruction wherever he went. She wasn't going to give him a chance to hurt Finn.

Holly pointed a finger at her father. "You stay away from him."

Her father's eyes widened with surprise. "But it's a father's place to make sure the guy is worthy of his daughter."

She clenched her hands. "And you would be an expert on character and integrity?"

"What's that supposed to mean?"

"I saw you—everybody saw you flirting with that young woman who's what? My age? How could you?"

"I didn't mean for it to happen."

"You never do."

Her father at least had the decency to grow red-faced. "You don't understand—"

"You're right. I don't. I have to go."

She rushed past her father. Suddenly the walls felt as though they were closing in on her and it was hard to breathe. She knew not to trust men. Her father had taught her that at an early age. And he'd reinforced that lesson tonight.

What made her think that Finn would be different? No, he wasn't a womanizer, but he was a man. And he only trusted her so far. Without complete trust, they had nothing.

Except the babies, which she'd never keep from him. But they didn't have to be together to coparent. Because she refused to end up like her mother and blindsided by a man.

The fairy tale was over.

It was time she got on with her life—without Finn.

She headed for the door, needing fresh air.

What in the world?

Finn had caught glimpses of Holly and Meryl with their heads together. His gut had churned. *Nothing good will come of that.*

He tried to get away from a couple of gentlemen, but they were his partners in an upcoming deal and he didn't want to offend them. But for every excuse he came up with to make his exit, they came up with a new aspect of their pending deal that needed further attention.

He should have forewarned Holly that Meryl would be here. But honestly, it slipped his mind. Between the news of the babies and then Holly's surprise holiday gathering at the penthouse, his thoughts were not his own these days.

He breathed easier when the women parted. But the next time he spotted Holly, she was having a conversation with her father and if the hand gestures and the distinct frown were anything to go by, it wasn't going well.

"Gentlemen, these are all great points. And I look forward to discussing them in great detail, but I promised my date I wouldn't work tonight."

The men admitted that they'd made similar promises to their wives. They agreed to meet again after the first of the year. With a shake of hands, they parted.

Finn turned around in time to witness Holly heading for the door. He took off after her, brushing off people with a smile and promising to catch up with them soon. It wasn't in him to be outright rude, but his sixth sense was telling him Holly's fast exit was not good—not good at all.

He rushed past the security guards posted at the entrance of the museum, past the impressive columns, and started down the flight of steps. Snow was starting to fall and Holly didn't have a coat. What was she thinking?

When he stepped on the sidewalk, his foot slipped on a patch of ice. He quickly caught his balance. He glanced to the left and then right. Which way had she gone?

And then he saw the shadow of a person. Was that her? He drew closer and realized the person was sitting on the sidewalk. His heart clenched. He took off at a sprint.

When he reached Holly's side, he knelt down. "Holly, are you all right?"

She looked up at him with a tear trailing down her cheek. "No. I'm not."

"Should I call an ambulance?"

"No." She sniffled. "I just need a hand up. I... I slipped on some ice."

"Are you sure it's okay if you stand? I mean, what about the babies?"

"Just give me your hand." He did as she asked.

Once she was on her feet, she ran her hands over her bare arms. He noticed the goose bumps, which prompted him to slip off his jacket and place it over her shoulders. "Thank you. But you need it."

"Keep it. I'm fine." He had so much adrenaline flooding through his system at that particular moment that he really didn't notice the cold.

"Do you want to go back inside?"

She lifted the skirt of her gown. "I don't think so. My heel broke."

He glanced down, finding her standing on one foot as the other heel had broken and slipped off her foot. Without a word, he retrieved the heel and handed to her. Then he scooped her up in his arms.

"Put me down! What are you doing?"

"Taking you home."

"Finn, stop. We need to talk."

"You're right. We do. But not out here in the cold."

CHAPTER TWENTY-TWO

So MUCH FOR making a seamless exit.

Holly sat on the couch in Finn's penthouse feeling ridiculous for falling on the ice and breaking her shoe. The lights on the Christmas tree twinkled as though mocking her with their festiveness. She glanced away.

She'd trusted Finn and yet things about him and his past kept blindsiding her. How was she ever supposed to trust him? How was she supposed to believe he'd never hurt her?

Falling in love and trusting another human was like a free fall and trusting that your parachute would open. Holly wasn't sure she had the guts to free-fall. Her thoughts strayed back to her father. She inwardly shuddered, remembering him flirting with that young woman, and then he didn't even deny he was having an affair with her. Her mother had trusted him and then her stepmother. It was to their utter detriment.

Finn rushed back in the room with a damp cloth. "Here. Let me have your hand."

She held her injured hand out to him. He didn't say anything as he gently cleaned her scrapes and then applied some medicated cream before wrapping a bit of gauze around it.

"Did you hurt anything else?"

"Besides my pride? No."

"I wish you'd have talked to me before you took off. Anything could have happened to you—"

"If you hadn't noticed, I'm a grown woman. I can take care of myself."

He arched a brow at her outburst.

"Hey, anyone can slip on ice," he said calmly. "I just wish

you'd have talked to me. Why did you leave? Was it Meryl? Did she say something to upset you?"

"No. Actually she didn't. Not directly."

"What is that supposed to mean?"

"Why didn't you tell me she would be there? That you still interact with her?"

He shrugged and glanced away. "I don't know. I didn't think of it."

"Really? Is that the same reason you didn't tell me you're the mastermind behind the Mistletoe Ball? That without you, there wouldn't be a ball?"

"I guess I should have said something. I didn't think it was a big deal. I wasn't keeping it a secret from you, but I've been distracted. If you haven't noticed, we're having twins."

"What else haven't you told me?" Her fears and insecurities came rushing to the surface. "What else don't I know about you that's going to blindside me?"

His facial features hardened. "I'm sure there's lots you don't know about me, just like there's a lot I don't know about you." When she refused to back down, he added, "Do you want me to start with kindergarten or will a detailed report about my last five years do?"

She glared at him for being sarcastic. Then she realized she deserved it. She was overreacting. She'd let her family dig into her insecurities and her imagination had done the rest.

"You know what? Never mind." Finn got up from the couch. "If you don't trust me, this is never going to work. Just forget this—forget us. I was wrong to think it could work."

Her heart ached as she watched him walk out of the room. She didn't even know the person she'd become. It was like she was once again that insecure little girl who realized her father had lied to her—learning that her father had secretly exchanged his current family for a new one. And now her father was about to do it again.

But Finn hadn't done that. He hadn't done anything but be sweet and kind. Granted, he might not be totally forth-coming at times, but it wasn't because he was out to deceive her or hurt her. She couldn't punish him for the wrongs her father had done to her over the years.

If she was ever going to trust a man with her heart—it would be Finn. Because in truth she did love him. She'd fallen for him that first night when he'd invited her here to his penthouse. He'd been charming and entertaining.

Now, when it looked like she was going to have it all—the perfect guy, the amazing babies and a happily-ever-after—she was pulling away. In the light of day, the depth of her love for Finn scared her silly. Her instinct was to back away fast—just like she was doing now. And if she wasn't careful, she'd lose it all. If she hadn't already.

Still wearing Finn's jacket, she wrapped her arms around herself. She inhaled the lingering scent of his spicy cologne mingled with his unique male scent. Her eyes drifted closed.

There had to be a way to salvage things. Maybe she could plead a case of pregnancy hormones. Nah. She had to be honest with him about her fears and hope he'd be willing to work through them with her.

It was then she noticed something poking her. There was something in his inner jacket pocket. She reached inside and pulled out not one but two packages of pacifiers. One was pink and one was blue. Happy tears blurred her eyes as she realized just how invested Finn was in their expanding fam-ily. She had to talk to him—to apologize.

She swiped at her eyes and got to her feet, heading for the kitchen.

CHAPTER TWENTY-THREE

W̲HAT WAS HE DOING?

Finn chastised himself for losing his cool with Holly. Every time she questioned him, she poked at his insecurities about being a proper husband and father. He had so many doubts about doing a good job. He didn't even know what being a husband and father entailed. All he knew was that he wanted to do his best by his family.

And he wasn't a quitter. He fought for the things he believed in. Sometimes he fought too long for his own good. But this was his family—there was no retreating. He would somehow prove to Holly—and most of all to himself—that he could be there for her and the babies through the good and the bad.

Certain in what he needed to do, he turned on his heels and headed back to the living room, hoping Holly hadn't made a quick exit. If she had, it wouldn't deter him. He would find her. He would tell her that he loved her. Because that was what it all boiled down to. He was a man who was head over heels in love with the mother of his children.

When he entered the living room, he nearly collided with Holly. He put his hands on her shoulders to steady her. "Where are you going in such a rush?"

"To find you. There's something I need to say."

"There's something I need to say to you, too."

At the same time, they said, "I'm sorry."

Finn had to be sure he heard her correctly. "Really?"

She nodded before she lifted up on her tiptoes and with her hands on either side of his face, she pulled him down to her. The kiss wasn't light or hesitant. Instead her kiss was heated and demanding. Need thrummed in his veins. He never wanted to let her go.

It'd be oh, so easy to dispense with words. His hands wrapped around her waist, pulling her soft curves to his hard planes. A moan grew in the back of his throat and he didn't fight it. Holly had to know all of the crazy things she did to his body, to his mind, to his heart.

But he wanted—no, he needed to clear the air between them. Christmas was in the air and it was the time for setting aside the past and making a new start. That was exactly what he wanted to do with Holly.

It took every fiber of his being to pull away from her embrace. Her beautiful eyes blinked and stared at him in confusion. It'd be so easy to pull her close again and pick up where they'd left off.

No, Finn. Do the responsible thing. Make this right for both of you.

"Come sit down so we can talk." He led her to the couch.

"Talk? Now?"

"Trust me. It's important."

"As long as I go first," she said. "After all, I started this whole thing."

"Deal."

She inhaled a deep breath and then blew it out. She told him about running into her family and how her father's actions and her stepsisters' words had ripped the scabs off her insecurities. "I know that's not a good excuse, but it's the truth. I've spent most of my life swearing that I would never end up like my mother—that I'd never blindly trust a man."

"And then you ran into my ex and found out I'd left out some important details about my life."

Holly shrugged and glanced away. "I just let it all get to me." She lifted her chin until her gaze met his. "I know you're not my father. You are absolutely nothing like him. I trust you."

"You do?"

She nodded. "I can't promise that every once in a while my insecurities won't get the best of me, but I promise to work on them."

"I love you, Holly."

Her eyes grew shiny with unshed tears. "I love you, too."

He cleared his throat, hoping his voice wouldn't fail him before he got it all out. "I would never intentionally hurt you or our children. You and those babies mean everything to me. I'm really excited to be a father."

"I noticed." She reached in his jacket pocket and pulled out the pacifiers. "I found these. And they're so sweet. Our babies' first gifts."

"You like them?"

She nodded. "How could I have ever doubted you?"

"I promise you here and now that I'll work on being more forthcoming. I've spent so many years keeping things bottled up inside me that I might slip up now and then. Will you stick by me while I work on this partnership thing?"

She nodded. "As long as you'll stick by me while I learn to let go of the past."

"It's a deal." Then recalling the flowers, he jumped to his feet. "I have something for you." He moved to the bookcase and retrieved the flowers. "I got these for you when I went to the pharmacy earlier." He held them out to her.

She accepted the bouquet and sniffed them. "They're beautiful."

This was his chance to make this Christmas unforgettable. He took her hand in his and gazed up into her wide-open eyes. "Holly, the most important thing you need to know about me is that I love you. And I love those babies you're carrying. I want to be the best husband and father, if you'll let me. Will you marry me?"

A tear splashed onto her cheek. She moved his hand to

her slightly rounded abdomen. "We love you, too. And yes. Yes! Yes! I'll marry you."

His heart filled with love—the likes he'd never known. And it was all Holly's doing. She'd opened his eyes and his heart not only to the spirit of the season, but also to the possibilities of the future.

He leaned forward, pressing his lips to hers.

This was the best Christmas ever.

EPILOGUE

THERE—THAT SHOULD do it.

Finn stepped back from the twelve-foot Christmas tree that stood prominently in front of the bay windows of his new house—correction, *their* house…as in his and Holly's home. This was the very first Christmas tree that he'd decorated since he was a child. Surprisingly it didn't hurt nearly as much as he'd thought. The memories of his brother and parents were always there, lingering around the edges, but now he was busy making new memories with Holly and their twins, Derek, in honor of his brother, and Maggie, in honor of his mother.

"How's it going?" Holly ventured into the room carrying a twin in each arm.

"I just finished putting on the lights. And how about you? Is Project Santa a go?"

Holly's face lit up. "Yes. And this year will be even bigger than last year, which means we're able to help even more children."

"I knew you were the right person to put in charge."

Maggie let out a cry. Holly bounced her on her hip. "Sounds like someone is hungry."

"Did I hear someone cry out for food?" Holly's mother strolled into the room, making a beeline for Maggie.

Finn glanced over at his mother-in-law, Sandy, who now lived in a mother-in-law apartment on the other side of their pool. When Holly had suggested her mother move in, he had to admit that he'd been quite resistant to the idea. But when Holly really wanted something, he found himself unable to say no.

In the end, he and Sandy hit it off. The woman was a lot

more laid-back than he'd ever imagined. And she doted over her grandchildren, which won her a gold star. And with the help of a nanny and a housekeeper, they were one big, happy family—unless of course the twins were hungry or teething.

"I can do it, Mom," Holly insisted, hanging on to the baby.

"Nonsense. I wasn't doing anything important." Sandy glanced over at the tree. "And from the looks of things in here, your husband could use some help."

Holly smiled. "I think you're right." She handed over the fussing baby. "Thanks. I'll be in shortly."

"Don't hurry. I've got this." Sandy started toward the kitchen. "Isn't that right, Maggie? We're buddies."

Holly stepped up beside Finn. "Are you sure you bought enough lights to cover all of the tree?"

"Yes. I'll show you." He bent over and plugged them in.

His wife arched a brow at him as though she knew something that he didn't. This was never a good sign.

"You should have tested them before putting them on the tree."

"What?" He turned around to find the top and middle of the tree all lit up, but the bottom section was dark. But how could that be? "I swear I tested them before I strung them."

Holly moved up next to him and handed over Derek. "Maybe it's just payback."

He glanced at his wife, trying to figure out what payback she was referring to. And then he recalled that last Christmas he'd shared the story of how he and his brother had swiped a strand of lights from the Christmas tree in order to light up their blanket fort.

A smile pulled at Finn's lips at the memory. It was the first time he'd been able to look back on his past and smile. That was all thanks to Holly. Her gift to him last year was giving his life back to him. Instead of walking around a shell of a man, he was taking advantage of every breath he had on this earth.

"Perhaps you're right. Maybe Derek's playing tricks on me."

"Did you hear that?" Holly leaned forward and tickled their son's tummy, making him giggle and coo. "Are you playing tricks on your daddy?"

Finn knew she was adding a bit of levity to the moment to keep things from getting too serious. Finn liked the thought that his brother might be looking down over them and smiling. Right here and now the past and the present came together, making Finn feel complete.

"Would you do that?" Finn placed his finger in his son's hand. "Would you steal the lights from the Christmas tree to make a fort?"

"Don't give him ideas," Holly lightly scolded. "I have a feeling your son will get into enough trouble of his own without any help from you."

"I think you might be right."

"And if he has a little brother, we'll really have our hands full."

This was the first time Holly had ever mentioned having another baby. It was usually him going on about expanding their family because to his surprise and delight, he loved being a dad. He'd even considered quitting the day job to be a full-time parent until Holly put her foot down and told him that someone had to keep the family business going to hand down to their children. But he no longer worked from morning till late at night. He took vacations and weekends. He had other priorities now.

"I think it'd be great to have another baby. Just let me know when you want my assistance. I'm all yours."

"Oh, you've done plenty already."

"Hey, what's that supposed to mean?" Derek wiggled in his arms. "Oh, you mean the twins? What can I say? When I do something I go all out."

"Well, let's just hope this time around I'm not carrying

twins or you might just be staying home to take care of all of them while I run the office."

Surely he'd misunderstood her. She couldn't be—could she? "Are...are you pregnant?"

She turned to him and with tears of joy in her eyes, she nodded. "Merry Christmas."

Finn whooped with joy before leaning forward and planting a kiss on his wife's lips. He'd never been so happy in his life. In fact, he never knew it was possible to be this happy.

"You give the best Christmas presents ever, Mrs. Lockwood."

"Well, Mr. Lockwood, you inspire me." She smiled up at him. "I love you."

"I love you the mostest."

* * * * *

MILLS & BOON®
Hardback – October 2016

ROMANCE

The Return of the Di Sione Wife	Caitlin Crews
Baby of His Revenge	Jennie Lucas
The Spaniard's Pregnant Bride	Maisey Yates
A Cinderella for the Greek	Julia James
Married for the Tycoon's Empire	Abby Green
Indebted to Moreno	Kate Walker
A Deal with Alejandro	Maya Blake
Surrendering to the Italian's Command	Kim Lawrence
Surrendering to the Italian's Command	Kim Lawrence
A Mistletoe Kiss with the Boss	Susan Meier
A Countess for Christmas	Christy McKellen
Her Festive Baby Bombshell	Jennifer Faye
The Unexpected Holiday Gift	Sophie Pembroke
Waking Up to Dr Gorgeous	Emily Forbes
Swept Away by the Seductive Stranger	Amy Andrews
One Kiss in Tokyo...	Scarlet Wilson
The Courage to Love Her Army Doc	Karin Baine
Reawakened by the Surgeon's Touch	Jennifer Taylor
Second Chance with Lord Branscombe	Joanna Neil
The Pregnancy Proposition	Andrea Laurence
His Illegitimate Heir	Sarah M. Anderson

MILLS & BOON®
Large Print – October 2016

ROMANCE

Wallflower, Widow...Wife!	Ann Lethbridge
Bought for the Greek's Revenge	Lynne Graham
An Heir to Make a Marriage	Abby Green
The Greek's Nine-Month Redemption	Maisey Yates
Expecting a Royal Scandal	Caitlin Crews
Return of the Untamed Billionaire	Carol Marinelli
Signed Over to Santino	Maya Blake
Wedded, Bedded, Betrayed	Michelle Smart
The Greek's Nine-Month Surprise	Jennifer Faye
A Baby to Save Their Marriage	Scarlet Wilson
Stranded with Her Rescuer	Nikki Logan
Expecting the Fellani Heir	Lucy Gordon

HISTORICAL

The Many Sins of Cris de Feaux	Louise Allen
Scandal at the Midsummer Ball	Marguerite Kaye & Bronwyn Scott
Marriage Made in Hope	Sophia James
The Highland Laird's Bride	Nicole Locke
An Unsuitable Duchess	Laurie Benson

MEDICAL

Seduced by the Heart Surgeon	Carol Marinelli
Falling for the Single Dad	Emily Forbes
The Fling That Changed Everything	Alison Roberts
A Child to Open Their Hearts	Marion Lennox
The Greek Doctor's Secret Son	Jennifer Taylor
Caught in a Storm of Passion	Lucy Ryder

MILLS & BOON®
Hardback – November 2016

ROMANCE

Di Sione's Virgin Mistress	Sharon Kendrick
Snowbound with His Innocent Temptation	Cathy Williams
The Italian's Christmas Child	Lynne Graham
A Diamond for Del Rio's Housekeeper	Susan Stephens
Claiming His Christmas Consequence	Michelle Smart
One Night with Gael	Maya Blake
Married for the Italian's Heir	Rachael Thomas
Unwrapping His Convenient Fiancée	Melanie Milburne
Christmas Baby for the Princess	Barbara Wallace
Greek Tycoon's Mistletoe Proposal	Kandy Shepherd
The Billionaire's Prize	Rebecca Winters
The Earl's Snow-Kissed Proposal	Nina Milne
The Nurse's Christmas Gift	Tina Beckett
The Midwife's Pregnancy Miracle	Kate Hardy
Their First Family Christmas	Alison Roberts
The Nightshift Before Christmas	Annie O'Neil
It Started at Christmas...	Janice Lynn
Unwrapped by the Duke	Amy Ruttan
Hold Me, Cowboy	Maisey Yates
Holiday Baby Scandal	Jules Bennett

MILLS & BOON®
Large Print – November 2016

ROMANCE

Di Sione's Innocent Conquest	Carol Marinelli
A Virgin for Vasquez	Cathy Williams
The Billionaire's Ruthless Affair	Miranda Lee
Master of Her Innocence	Chantelle Shaw
Moretti's Marriage Command	Kate Hewitt
The Flaw in Raffaele's Revenge	Annie West
Bought by Her Italian Boss	Dani Collins
Wedded for His Royal Duty	Susan Meier
His Cinderella Heiress	Marion Lennox
The Bridesmaid's Baby Bump	Kandy Shepherd
Bound by the Unborn Baby	Bella Bucannon

HISTORICAL

The Unexpected Marriage of Gabriel Stone	Louise Allen
The Outcast's Redemption	Sarah Mallory
Claiming the Chaperon's Heart	Anne Herries
Commanded by the French Duke	Meriel Fuller
Unbuttoning the Innocent Miss	Bronwyn Scott

MEDICAL

Tempted by Hollywood's Top Doc	Louisa George
Perfect Rivals...	Amy Ruttan
English Rose in the Outback	Lucy Clark
A Family for Chloe	Lucy Clark
The Doctor's Baby Secret	Scarlet Wilson
Married for the Boss's Baby	Susan Carlisle